元2

2

Praise for Turducken:

"*Turducken* is an energ
bizarre, and the com
ability to constantly surprise from genre to genre is a
rare pleasure. Her stories masterfully play with form
and reader expectations at every turn, until you
almost feel less like a reader and more like a
passenger in her wicked car, or a guest at her
banquet, and you've got no choice but to buckle up,
settle in, and eat hearty."

— K.C. Mead-Brewer, Pushcart Prize-nominated, and Best of
the Net-nominated author

"Lindz McLeod's short story collection, *Turducken*, is
as rich and vivid in its language and imagery as it is
experimental. The stories within this collection are
smart and quirky and often use cheeky metaphors to
illuminate complex and unique relationship dynamics
which highlight McLeod's careful observation and
details of intimate life and living. Many of the stories
use the backdrop of Edinburgh and hone in on its
culture and gothic landscape. McLeod uses the
metaphorical to understand the literal, featuring
humans as places and as creatures—the collection is
psychological, primal, satirical, haunting, and gut-
wrenching."

— Ai Jiang, author of *Linghun* and *Ai Jiang's Smol Tales From
Between Worlds*, and Nebula Award for Best Short Story
Nominee for "Give Me English"

"Clear prose and a bright vision, Lindz McLeod's new story collection, *Turducken*, is much like the title creature, containing multitudes. There is a perfect balance of humor/the weird/horror in these separate pieces with themes that subtly intersect and echo back to each other – well rendered domestic scenes that go off the rails in a wonderful array of surprising directions."

— Jeffrey Ford, World-Fantasy, Nebula, and Edgar Allan Poe award-winning author of *The Drowned Life, A Natural History of Hell* and many more

"*Turducken* is an eclectic and boisterous mix of the dark and mysterious, the fantastical, the sardonic and the real. It is a collection that I would advise any keen literary aficionado to add with haste to their collection of literary works. I am beyond honoured to have had the pleasure of reading this riveting collection and only hope that you, dear reader, cherish *Turducken* as much as I do!"

— A. R. Arthur, *Full House Literary* (fullhouseliterary.com)

Turducken

Lindz McLeod

Denver, Colorado

Published in the United States by:
Spaceboy Books LLC
1627 Vine Street
Denver, CO 80206
www.readspaceboy.com

First printed June 2023

ISBN: 978-1-951393-22-9

To the turducken, without whom the title for this collection would probably be something quite normal.

CONTENTS

TURDUCKEN

(published by Baffling Mag)

alfway through peeling the carrots for
Sunday lunch, Petey announced he'd bred a
turducken. The kitchen, busy with humdrum
small talk and the chop of various knives, fell
immediately silent.

"You mean you've brought one?" Our mother,
hands still wet from washing, glanced from the
already full oven to my brother and back again.

Petey didn't bring anything. When he arrived two
hours ago I watched him stamping through the front
door, not bothering to wipe his boots. A trail of wet,
orange leaves behind him like a comet tail. Nothing in
his hands, not even a bottle of wine.

"No, Ma." He wiped the back of his hand over his forehead. "I mean I finally figured it out."

"How in the hell—" Da opened and closed his mouth, searching for words that never arrived.

I put down my paring knife. "How many cloacas does it have?"

Petey scowled. "One, obviously. It was more efficient that way."

Da sank into the nearest chair. "How many hearts?"

"Three. They each need their own. The earlier models didn't survive."

Lunch was swiftly abandoned; we piled into two cars and drove to Petey's house. Past the barn where his lone horse was stabled, we followed him towards a fenced-off enclosure. Despite myself, I was curious. As he swung the door to a little shed open, the pale daylight illuminated a creature only a little wider than an ordinary turkey. The feathers had been shaved away on the front and sides of the bird; strange bulges rippled and pushed beneath the skin, as if it were pregnant. On the beast's back, dark feathers—brown, tipped with cream—bristled against the faint breeze. The tail was a magnificent fan, typical of the species. I'd expected it to look more pathetic, or more monstrous. More like a frankenchicken. Instead, it just looked like a bloated turkey.

"Oh," Da said, sounding a little disappointed. "I

thought they'd be on the outside, for some reason."

"Sweetheart, think critically," Ma chided. "The chicken is inside the duck which is in turn inside the turkey. That's how they're cooked, right?" She clapped a hand over her mouth. "Wait. It can't talk, can it? I shouldn't have said anything about cooking."

"No, Ma, it's just a bird."

The creatures' beady eyes were fixed on my mother and—although they were glazed over—something about its body suggested it was listening closely to every word.

"You're playing God, son. I don't know about this." Da stroked his beard.

"Oh Michael," Ma said, exasperated. "When old Mrs Patterson told us she got Lasik you said she was playing God. When I brought home candyfloss grapes for the first time you said we were playing God. Didn't stop you from eating them."

"I stand by my point." He didn't directly address the grapes, though, so we all knew he'd lost the argument.

I leaned closer, staring into the beast's beady little eyes, watching the red wattle wobble as it jerked this way and that. "What do you feed it? Swans?"

My brother sniffed. "That would be inhumane, Claire."

"You're the one who bred a turducken, bro."

"Children," Ma said. "Perhaps the bickering could wait until after lunch?"

3

Lunch from Petey's fridge consisted of half a stale loaf and a wad of dubious prosciutto, the origins of which were never verified to my satisfaction. After eating, if one could call it that, I stepped outside with my mother, who had a cigarette already dangling from her lips. I pulled my smokes out.

"Can I get a match?"

She patted her pockets to no avail. "I could have sworn I put the box right back in my pocket. Here." She took my cigarette and lit it from her own, passing the genetic cherry down the family tree.

"What do you think of this? I mean, really?"

"I think we should support your brother, darling."

"Don't you think it's screwed up?"

"I think," she blew a ring of smoke, "it's a good thing that he's not into drugs and gang crime. And I think we should be grateful that he has a hobby."

I stared at the little shed. I could just see the head of the turducken, bobbing around inside. "Do you think he's playing God?"

She considered this. "I think there are worse people to aspire to be."

✳

Bigheart know where food and how to mate. Bigheart know danger, what to peck, when to run and flap.

Middleheart know water. Middleheart always want water—on feet, on body feathers. Middleheart say *fish taste good, paddle feel so good, please water water water please.*

Smallheart has little fast thoughts like eggs cracking. Smallheart know lots. Smallheart say *we* and *think* and *escape.*

Bigheart want to please Man Who Feed. Middleheart want to please Man Who Feed. Smallheart don't want to please Man Who Feed.

Smallheart say *danger* and *fly* and *freedom.* Bigheart don't recognize any of those words. Middleheart only think about *diving down, green, fish fish fish.*

Bigheart content to stay inside. Middleheart see pond, want to swim. Smallheart say *now, a chance.*

Three stretch wings wide. Three slide peg up with beak. Smallheart say *yes, that.* Bigheart like outside. Middleheart pulls towards pond. Smallheart say *not yet.* Middleheart quack. Bigheart feel Middleheart peck inside. Bigheart hurt. Smallheart say *one thing, then bigger pond.* Middleheart say *yes? big pond fish please? Please pond?*

Smallheart say *promise.* Middleheart silent. Middleheart don't know *promise.* Bigheart trust Smallheart. Three approach Man Who Feed nest. Smallheart say *here* and *box* and *fire.* Bigheart peck at box, no fire. Smallheart say, *scratch with claw.* Three lift foot and scratch box. Sparks fly. Three watch dry grass catch fire. Three watch red fire wriggle towards Man Who Feed nest. Smallheart say *yes* and *good* and *revenge.* Smallheart say *walk quick, walk now, walk away.*

Three waddle until Man Who Feed nest look small. Three walk until sun hot on feathers. Smallheart say *well done, go further.* Bigheart tired. Three tired. Three walk until no sun. Smallheart say *further.* Three walk until *smell of green, big roar, yellow sand.*

Middleheart say *now pond?*

Smallheart so sad. Smallheart say *now pond.*

THEM AT NUMBER SEVENTY-FOUR

(published by Pseudopod)

hen body number four is discovered, Mrs Patterson thinks that surely now she and her husband will be caught. Days creep past, then a week.

Two.

Three.

Their excitement and relief begins to fade. Once again, the desire blossoms, delicate at first, but growing bolder as the hours and days pass. Over a dinner of chips, peas, and gammon steaks, Mrs Patterson ventures a suggestion that perhaps it's time they do another. Her husband chews for a moment, points out that there's another James Bond marathon on this weekend they won't want to miss. She cedes the point. Seeing her disappointment, he suggests he can't rule out the possibility they might kill again sooner, if someone suitable pops up. *Play it by ear,* he says. *Pass the salt, please.*

On Thursday afternoon, Mr and Mrs Patterson have resigned themselves to an early evening. They're driving towards Aldi to pick up breakfast items—soft, white bread, margarine, sausages, and eggs. Tonight, they weren't planning to do more than order a Chinese takeaway and have a glass of red wine while watching Gogglebox, but as their car passes the petrol station, Mrs Patterson glimpses dark hair—wild, untamed, unparted, as if Moses had never even heard of the sea—and something snaps. She pats her husband's arm and he swerves instantly, parking on the other side of the road. Mrs Patterson points at the young woman striding into the station. They wait until she emerges again, tugging the collar of her faded denim jacket up against the wind, and slides back into her blue Kia.

They follow her in the car for a couple of miles, staying a respectable distance behind. The Kia shudders into the driveway of a semi-detached house. The young woman carries a tattered, bulging shopping bag from the boot into the house. She reuses plastic bags— that's good for the environment. Mr and

Mrs Patterson are religious about the reuse of plastic bags.

They cruise along the street, peering out at the house. Only one car in the driveway. No toys in the garden. *An absence of children.* The grass is a little overgrown, with a few weeds swaying in the wind. *An absence of husband.* They park at the end of the terrace and pretend to study a paper map. Mrs Patterson points out that the house is the last one on the end of a terrace, which provides easier access from the road, as well as reducing the amount of potential witnesses who might hear a struggle. Mr Patterson notes the lack of security cameras or neighborhood watch signs. He drums his fingers on the steering wheel. *Looking good. Can't be too careful, though,* he says, and Mrs Patterson agrees.

After making a mental note of the house's location, they return home. They consult the map again—flimsy, thin paper, easily destroyed, should they ever need to dispose of such a thing quickly—to determine whether or not the house is too close to their own home. It's close; cutting it very fine, but Mr Patterson thinks it will be suitable. Mrs Patterson is more cautious. She was the one who spotted the young woman, and while she's keen to bond with her husband again, she's reluctant to dabble with danger. They decide to mull it over. Mr Patterson places an order with the local Chinese restaurant over the phone, and while they're waiting for it to arrive, they switch the TV over to Countdown. *A consonant please, Rachel*, Mrs Patterson mouths along with contestant A, and frowns when contestant A requests a fourth vowel. *Far too many. Three's all you need.*

Mr Patterson concurs. *Four is greedy. Over-egging the pudding.*

Subsequently, Contestant A overreaches, and is soundly beaten by contestant B. When it's time for the numbers game, Mrs Patterson stares vacantly into space and tries to picture what the young woman's home decor looks like, while Mr Patterson solves the game out loud and gets within one digit of the correct answer. When the host shows her working on the whiteboard, he sighs and berates himself for missing a trick. Mrs Patterson consoles him.

They peck on the lips. The takeaway arrives moments later.

On Friday night, clad in dark clothes, they slip out of the back door and under the loose piece of fence. The hills between their village and the slightly larger town are pockmarked with warrens; they move at a steady pace, smothered in starlight. It takes them just under an hour to get to the house. Mrs Patterson uses a small lock-picking kit—an excellent bargain from a local charity shop—to unlock the back door.

They sidle inside, checking each room carefully before entering. On the ground floor, the lights are off. A cursory examination of the living room proves there are no toys littering the carpet, nor any chew sticks or bones. The shoe rack by the front door contains only one size of shoe. The jackets hanging on the pegs are feminine. Mr and Mrs Patterson watch a lot of crime shows and they have learned several important lessons: do not check out the crime scene beforehand, do not return to it afterwards for any reason, get in quickly and get out quicker. Do not photograph or otherwise film the house or victim. Leave your mobile phone at home lest the police use location data to track you.

The young woman is upstairs. Footsteps creak on the landing. As soft slipper-treads can be heard on the stairs, Mr Patterson offers Mrs Patterson the opportunity to strike first. She declines. She did the last one. Fair is fair.

They stand either side of the kitchen door. The young woman makes it precisely one step inside before Mr Patterson stabs her. After the knife slides in and out again, the young woman judders a couple of times, collapses face-down onto the floor, and stills. A faint bubbling, probably a collapsing lung. Red tinging her lips. Not much fanfare, but then again, they aren't dramatic people.

Mrs Patterson wouldn't say they're professionals. Not at all—very amateur, in fact, although she'd admit that they're both keen enough to improve—but after the fifth time, something shining and golden emanates from both of them as they stand over the body of the young woman. Glancing around, Mr Patterson remarks on how clean the grouting is between the kitchen tiles. Mrs Patterson agrees, and adds that the skirting boards are likewise free from dust and grime. *Kept a nice house, so she did.* They stare down at the body, and hold hands like they did when they were courting. Tightly, with coiled, anticipatory energy.

They're back home in just enough time for a rerun of Pointless.

On Saturday, they do some gardening. Mrs Patterson loves her hanging baskets. When the storm comes, the rain pelts the flowers, knocking petals and leaves to the ground with casual cruelty. Mrs Patterson watches, tears brimming in her eyes, until Mr Patterson braves the wind, fleece pulled over his head, and slides the babies under the patio table to shelter them.

Dinner is a shop-bought lasagna and garlic bread. Dessert is fruit, because Mrs Patterson thinks her favourite jeans are getting a bit tight around the waist again. Mr Patterson, whose expanding and contracting stomach is rarely a source of consternation for him, dutifully agrees to commit to a diet in solidarity.

Television is good on a Saturday night. They watch all their favourite shows and in between, relive the memories of the previous night. They compare the kill to the others in minute detail; Mrs Patterson's favourite was the second, because she felt that the first one was a bit of a faff, especially when the victim wriggled out of Mr Patterson's grip and almost escaped. Mr Patterson agrees that the second kill was cleaner than the first, but admits that the fourth kill was his favourite. *Why is that*, Mrs Patterson wants to know. *Because it was the first time you smiled afterwards*, he says. She rolls her eyes. *Oh, you're an old romantic.*

You know you love it, he says.

On Sunday their son comes for dinner with his fiancee. Mrs Patterson cooks a beautiful roast chicken and juliennes carrots while Mr Patterson ably handles the creamy mashed potatoes and makes the same old jokes about lumpy gravy. During dinner, the fiancee compliments the food, the house. Mr And Mrs Patterson like her immensely. The conversation switches to celebrities. Their son makes a reference to the time a high profile comedian cheated on his high profile actress wife. For a long moment, the only sound is the scrape and clink of cutlery. The fiancee doesn't notice. Later, when the son and his fiancee leave, Mrs Patterson does not bring up this moment. Instead, she puts on the kettle and busies herself with wiping the countertops. Mr Patterson assumes it's best left alone. He pours milk into the mugs, then dries the dishes while the tea brews.

They hold hands on the sofa, watching a chat

show host interview an actress about an upcoming science fiction film they'll never see. Afterwards, they watch the first twenty minutes of a film, before realising they are too tired to continue. They brush their teeth together, recounting the evening's events. The conversation leads, as it frequently does, into a brief discussion of the son's previous girlfriends. As always, they decide that some were more tolerable than others but the fiancee is easily the best, prettiest, kindest, most well-suited one. Their son seems very happy; this pleases them. The decision soothes them with its familiarity.

Mr and Mrs Patterson kiss goodnight and go to bed in separate rooms—he snores, she has restless legs, and they firmly believe that one of the keys to a successful is marriage is a good night's sleep.

On Monday, Mr Patterson plays squash with ex-colleagues. Mrs Patterson has lunch with two long-standing friends, then spends an hour swimming the calories off in the local pool. At home, they have a coffee and catch up on the events of the day. Dinner is leftover roast chicken and chips. Dessert is clementines, which Mr Patterson peels and divides into segments, eaten during The Chase. By the time Who Wants To Be A Millionaire is on, they're ready for another coffee. Mr Patterson answers several questions incorrectly in order to make Mrs Patterson laugh. They retire to bed, pleased with their productivity.

On Tuesday, their daughter phones for her usual weekly chat and inquires after their security measures. Mr Patterson assures her that they lock the doors carefully every night and have an alarm system. Their daughter mentions the recent murders. Mrs Patterson repeats her carefully rehearsed lines about the victims; all different genders, sexualities, and races. No known links between them. The daughter persists, but as soon as Mrs Patterson begins to quote the Sun newspaper, she changes the subject by habit, as they knew she would. They finish up the phone call with cheery goodbyes, safe in the knowledge that they are the last people in the world who would be suspected of such crimes. They were witnesses at their gay neighbours' civil union over a decade prior. They frequently lend a hand in the bi-annual village fair, although they do prefer to keep to themselves. They're frequently seen on the nearby hills, walking Mrs Patterson's sister's beautiful Alsatian. Mrs Patterson would like to have a dog, but Mr Patterson has pointed out that a dog restricts your freedom.

Mrs Patterson likes to feel free while staying firmly in her comfort zone, so a dog is off the table. For now.

On Wednesday, they drive out to the shopping centre and have tea and scones before browsing the clothing stores.

Mrs Patterson wonders how they ever got so much done before they retired. Mr Patterson reiterates the point, detailing how every day seems so full of activity. She does not mind that he remakes her points as if they were his own; conversely, she feels rather important that by producing a baseline, she can encourage him to embellish, to make something bolder and more exuberant. She likes being his foundation, and she is happy to believe she is more of a backstage person.

Several years ago, when their marriage had been rocky, other people had plenty of suggestions: counselling, couples retreats, all that new age mumbo jumbo. After weeks of talking it over, they decided all they needed was a fresh start. A proper clean slate. A new shared hobby. They'd been watching a BBC box set—some Danish crime drama, which Mr Patterson wasn't particularly keen on because of the subtitles— when the idea had struck both of them at the same time. An exchange which at any time might have been superfluous and easily forgotten had caused a sudden spark of interest.

At first, simply talking about the plan had been enough to bring them closer together. Yet they'd craved more; more intimacy, more physicality. Past middle age, they wanted to create memories. Experiences. Adventures beyond frequent holidays to the Spanish and Portuguese islands. The first victim had almost been their last, but things had worked out perfectly. No one was any the wiser, and the marriage was stronger than ever. As the rain drums a blues rhythm against the conservatory windows, Mrs Patterson thinks that, all in all, it was really rather perfect.

On Thursday, Mrs Patterson goes to the post office to pay their bills. In the queue, she listens to two elderly women discussing the murders. *They'll catch him*, one says. *No doubt in my mind. They all get caught in the end.* Mrs Patterson busies herself by admiring the range of holiday and occasion greeting cards, and selects a couple of suitable options to keep in the stash at home, in case she has forgotten to pop any upcoming birthdays or anniversaries in the diary. She wonders why people always assume a murderer is a man, and why they think he has to be working alone. She and Mr Patterson are different. They're a team, she thinks, and is comforted by the idea.

When she returns, Mr Patterson makes tea and ham sandwiches. Afterwards, they each have two chocolate digestive biscuits, and discuss how long they should wait before killing again. He thinks it might be sensible to strike immediately but hide this body in a more secure location than the last. He suggests a local wooded area. Mrs Patterson blinks, puzzled. She points out that they hid body number four there and it was found far too quickly. He stares down at the map and hesitates before stabbing a spot with a thick finger. *There.* It's a fine suggestion.

Mrs Patterson puts the kettle on again.

The next couple of weeks are quiet. Another storm wrecks the flowerbeds and baskets, so they make several trips to the garden centre to replace the ruined ones. Mr Patterson drives past the usual turn without indicating. Mrs Patterson nudges him, wondering if he'd been so enthralled with the latest chart-topper on the radio that he'd failed to notice. He double-takes, turns at the next roundabout, and swings back onto the correct road. It's not the first time he's done this over the last few years, but it's the first time he's got lost on a road they travel weekly. Mrs Patterson questions him but he insists he's fine, simply a little tired. She ceases her questions when his tone takes on an ugly edge. A scarlet streak adorns his cheekbones. His eyes stay firmly on the road.

Driving back from their favourite restaurant, two towns over, Mr Patterson takes a winding back road that Mrs Patterson is unfamiliar with. She shifts in her seat, wondering why he didn't stick to the well-lit and peopled main road. For the first time, the awareness of the items packed neatly in their trunk—black bags, shovels, one large sterilised knife, hand sanitiser, spare towel—rings an uncomfortable warning. She'd chosen and purchased each of them, yet she'd never quite comprehended the enormity of their presence. The road is lined with unclothed trees, branches shivering in the darkness. She slides cold fingers onto Mr Patterson's knee, and is relieved to see him glance over, smiling, as if the thought had never crossed his mind. She's heard of partners turning on each other, of course—it happens all the time on television. Not to them, though. Mr and Mrs Patterson are different. A true team, tried and tested. She gives him an extra kiss before bed, just to be sure.

On a windy Monday, Mr Patterson asks her twice where the jam is kept. He's baffled when she gently suggests that there might be something wrong, and angry once he realizes what she's getting at. He doesn't need a doctor. He's still in the prime of life.

In their usual supermarket, he checks each aisle's title—Chilled Meats, Frozen Meats, Home Goods—before committing to perusing the shelves. Mrs Patterson notices this new habit, but has the sense not to address it immediately.

The following week, during a news broadcast of their latest victim, Mrs Patterson peeks around the kitchen door and watches him search through the cupboards again for the jam. It takes him four cupboards before he locates the jar, by which time his bushy eyebrows are kissing in confusion. Lying in bed alone, listening to the silence of the house, Mrs Patterson considers the possibilities. Wracking her brain, she's certain the jars have been kept in the same cupboard since time immemorial. The jam is, therefore, indicative of a larger problem.

Mrs Patterson rarely puts her foot down about anything, so it comes as a shock to Mr Patterson when he realizes she isn't going to budge. Tears are the final nail in the coffin; he presses her close to his chest and kisses the top of her head. He agrees to see a doctor.

Mr Patterson is given a thorough examination and booked in for an MRI, which he finds oppressive and strange. Afterwards, the doctor talks them through the results of the scan. Defiant, Mr Patterson argues that he feels fine, this can't really be all that bad. The doctor has seen more than her fair share of elderly patients. She remains calm and patient. The news begins to sink in.

At home again, in the place where they feel most comfortable, Mr and Mrs Patterson hold hands on the couch. The television has been turned off. Alexa is silent. The only sound is their own breathing, mirrored by the wind outside like the heaving breath of a dying god.

Mr Patterson suggests another outing to cheer them up; Mrs Patterson agrees, and excuses herself to the bathroom before they begin to draw up plans. Life has once again changed shape under her hands. She does not allow herself to cry. Not yet. She flushes the toilet to make the visit seem realistic, and splashes her face with cold water. She must adapt to a new challenge. Teamwork means making sacrifices; she is very used to ceding her own desires in favour of a joint endeavour. What she wants is to keep Mr

Patterson with her forever, regardless of his capacity. What they need is quite different. He is, through no fault of his own, a liability now. If it were her, he would reason through things in exactly the same way. He's always been a very practical man.

She stares into the mirror. The woman looking back knows that her next kill will be her last. She'll let him believe they have something exciting to look forward to. She'll remind him that he has been her whole world, and their marriage has been strengthened by their choices. Love is a verb—or so they say. There won't be any sudden movements, or black bags, or shovels. Just a soft slide into darkness, as easy and painless as falling asleep. It's the best and last gift she can give him.

After all, Mrs Patterson loves Mr Patterson.

PARADISE REGAINED

(published by Bear Creek)

He is a cruelly handsome man, with eyes like Brad Pitt and a mouth like a massacre. She is a cruelly beautiful woman, with hair like Sofia Vergara and eyes like late-stage syphilis. I sit between them on their unstained, margarine-soft leather couch, and sip my red wine as if this is a perfectly normal Thursday evening.

"What do you think of the wine?" He smiles.

"I have more dead relatives and lovers than seems plausible, even for rapidly-industrialising Victorian London." I clutch the stem of my glass, fur rippling with anticipation.

The woman rolls her eyes. "Ken, we've been over

this. She can only talk in Philip Pullman plot lines. She was extremely clear about it in her bio, weren't you darling?"

"I've just received an anonymous letter warning me to avoid something which is ambiguously named." I nod. "I immediately begin searching for it."

"Sorry." Ken's eyes rake my body. "So, how are we going to do this?"

I put my glass down and turn to the woman. "You are a kindly authority figure who has given a powerful, priceless and unique artefact to a pre-pubescent child," my webbed fingers trace the line of her jaw slowly, confidently, "who has no far shown no aptitude for anything other than achieving maximum grubbiness." I lean in for my best approximation of a kiss. My feathers are already fanning out and I can feel Ken's warm hands stroking the stub of my smooth tail. "You give the child minimal instructions on its use and no information on its value." I shoot him a coy look over my shoulder as he unbuckles his belt. "You expect this to turn out just fine."

He grips me harder around what he probably thinks of as my torso. "Emelie," he purrs, but there's no need. She's already unzipped her dress.

"My anatomy is absurd and leaves no room for a functioning nervous system."

"That's so hot," Emelie unclasps her bra.

They prove fast learners. By the time we make it into the bedroom, my wings are buzzing. Sharp clip-

clip-clips punctuate the smacking of mouths and the sound of feathers pressing against flesh.

I dig my claws into Ken's back as he thrusts. "I'm a thinly-veiled metaphor for the early Catholic church," I pant. He begins to speed up so I dig in harder, despite his wincing. "No, thinner than that."

His smile is half-smug, half-agonized as he keeps the steady pace. He drops his face into the crook of my long neck, nuzzling, as I tilt my beak back towards Emelie. She's a fine human specimen—they both are—but her eyes are full of a presence I've rarely felt before. She never closes them to kiss, and her shuddering brings me closer to a meandering climax.

When I finish, I spray my orange eggs towards the tarp on the floor. They'd been warned preemptively and I'm pleased to see they followed my instructions to the letter. After the younglings hatch, their freshly-sharpened claws tend to wreck hardwood floors. Much better to take them down to the beach and let them loose there.

I settle back against Ken's chest. "I'm chasing an absent father figure but when I eventually find him, after herculean efforts, my only reward will be the bitter taste of truth."

"The dating scene is hell, we know," Emelie flops onto her stomach, raking a hand through the soft down of my stomach. I trill with surprise and delight.

"I think I speak for both of us," Ken says, watching Emelie's face, "when I say that was fantastic and we'd love to see you again sometime."

"Absolutely," she says, without a moment's hesitation.

I grin, warmth spreading through my chest. "I am God and I wish to die."

CIPHER

(published by Catapult)

ACROSS

5. The way your friends now hesitate before getting changed in front of you, even though it's been years and you've held their hair back while they vomited cheap beer, seen them nude apart from heavy mascara and one sock, tucked them into your spare bed after their boyfriends cheated or threw vases or vacillated about having children just long enough to keep them on the hook forever. Your ex-husband's insecurities about whether or not he exudes "feminine energy" now that he knows about your proclivities, your preferences, your oscillations; the way he considers all men angles and all women hourglasses and never once acknowledges that women, too, can be sharp, can be compass points and broken glass and slatted blades, stacked forever. (10) ~~PROJECTION~~

7. One of the problems with divorce. Merged assets— once whisked together—are not so easily separated, much like the ingredients of a cake. Treasured memories and possessions divided into fractions. The career change you've been considering, now unsupported. (8) ~~FINANCES~~

9. It's not just a river in Egypt! (6) ~~DENIAL~~

10. Start with a compliment. Progress with your name, written in foam, backlit by chocolate sprinkles. Advance into regular hugs. Climax with a stolen kiss, no heavier than a shadow. What's necessary, in order to move forward. (7) ~~EMBRACE~~

DOWN

1. The color of stasis. A stolid refusal to upturn your entire life. Cowardice, in the face of reality. (6) PURPLE? ORANGE? ~~YELLOW~~

2. _____ Stewart, queer actress you feel like you should be attracted to but aren't. (6) LAUREN?

3. Times you've cried listening to "Body and Mind" by Girl in Red. (3, 8) ~~ONE THOUSAND~~

4. Therapy, peeling back years of repression, unwinding your skin like a mottled orange; compartmentalization is grainy-sweet, tempting in the same way as taking the first bite of someone else's birthday cake—you shouldn't, but god, wouldn't it taste so fucking good to bite into a fresh landscape? You want to say those words back to your girlfriend, the words she makes a gift of—not showy, or ostentatious, but a gift nonetheless—to make a trophy of your tongue, to hammer gold into curved, melodic notes and spread them on the floor like stepping stones into your chest. You can't, not yet. But you will. (10) ~~INEVITABLE~~

6. Consider the possibility of leaving your husband. Daydream about that pretty green-eyed barista with the long blonde hair. Contemplate what people might say when they gossip about you. Think about doing it anyway. (6) PONDER? ~~WONDER~~

8. Penguin flesh. Icebergs as metaphors for queer microaggressions; guys leering at your held hands on the street, catcalling as if you're nothing more than two sock puppets pushing your dry-heel empty-mouths together for their entertainment and pleasure. Your new girlfriend's feet during the night.

Your ex-mother-in-law's smile. (7) ~~GLACIAL~~

9. War among the gods. Conflict between duty and dreams. Also: a place where you can organize political protests and share information about new Kate Winslet movies and cute memes and engagement photos you once thought impossible. (7) ~~DISCORD~~

CITY BOYS IN COUNTRY CLOTHES

After the match finishes with a disappointing draw, Scottie suggests pre-gaming at Jeremy's, since his flat is closest to the Grassmarket. Others chime in with their agreement and they end up stopping into damn near every off-license on the way. The more economically-sound members of the pack carry blue plastic bags full of clinking craft beers. Hoyt walks at the tail-end of the group, balancing an eighteen-pack of Pilsners on his shoulder. An overestimate of his own drinking skills, obviously, but the guy behind the counter had said they were on sale and it seemed stupid to pay ten quid for nine when he could get twice as much for only fifteen.

As the clock approaches midnight, tensions rise over a first-person shooter. They're getting antsy, but nobody mentions leaving until Scottie stands up and stretches. They muddle down the dank stairwell, jostling and jeering. The night air is cool against Hoyt's skin. His aftershave stings under his chin where he nicked himself shaving earlier; not a deep cut, but a noticeable inch-long scratch. When Gaz notices and starts doing a Macauley Culkin impression, clapping hands to his cheeks and mock-screaming, Hoyt takes the ribbing with good cheer.

Outside the club, they don't have to queue for long. It's loud as hell, even by regular Edinburgh standards, but they find a just-vacated table near the door which happens to be the farthest from any of the speakers. A plump blonde—maybe a six underneath all that eyeliner, maybe a five in the harsh light of day—tosses her hair in Hoyt's direction a few times, but he plays it cool while nodding along to Grimsby, who's been screaming in his ear about FIFA regulations for the last twenty minutes. The floor is sticky underfoot and they're only making it worse. Pedro's devised some sort of splashy drinking game, and a couple of the lads are participating eagerly. Half the beer ends up on the floor and the bouncer has to tell them twice to calm down a bit. Scottie, his dark hair slicked back, black muscle shirt waxing and waning over his chiseled body, has promised they'll behave. Scottie, with his perfect teeth, high cheekbones, and effortless perfume-advert stubble, speaks quietly, and the lads subside with no more than a couple of eye rolls. If you ask any of them, they'll say the group doesn't have a leader. Not as such. Not per se. None of them would ever admit to being anything so beta as a mere follower. At least, that's what they'd say if Scottie wasn't in the room, because the guy exudes the kind of charisma you could never hope to emulate in a million years and have to pretend you don't envy. Not at all. Not one bit.

On Hoyt's right, the tequila shots are coming thick and fast as bullets; the sharp tang of lime mixes with whatever CK number Callum has liberally doused himself in. On his left, Scottie's looking past Pedro's shoulder at the fittest girl on the dancefloor, and she's looking right back at him.

Hoyt isn't bad with girls—none of them are, really —but Scottie's on a different level. He swigs his beer, never taking his eyes off the girl, and when she beckons him over, he hesitates. Checks his watch even though it's only quarter past one and Hoyt saw him check it only a few minutes earlier. The move is enough for the girl's smile to falter briefly, but when he shrugs and pushes through the crowd towards her, Hoyt watches her plump, shiny lips form the words *oh my god* to her friend, all silver woo-woo bangles and flailing arms, who gyrates to a respectful distance several feet away.

Scottie descends the three steps onto the smokey

pit. Flows like he's made of water, atoms folding around the girl one moment, pouring away in the next. She pushes back onto his body and grabs his hands. Puts them on her hips as she moves with the beat. Hoyt tilts his beer but it's empty already. He looks down at the green forest of glass, mossing over the white plastic table, covering almost every inch, and suddenly has an urge to sweep it clear with one stroke. The noise would be drowned completely by the thump-thump of the bass. He wants to watch something shatter. It's that kind of night.

Gaz taps him on the shoulder and passes him a cold beer. Right on time. He digs deep, hands over a tenner, but Gaz waves it away. Hoyt takes a long swill. A crumb of something brushes his tongue. Salt, maybe, left over from the tequila. He's swallowed it down before he can register what that means, if it means anything. Scottie's still dancing with the girl, mouth dipping to press against her neck, but something is parting the waves of dark-headed dancers. A thick, bald skull, aiming for Scottie like a shark. Hoyt's halfway to the dancefloor by the time the bouncer punches. Scottie ducks at the last moment, jostled by another dancer waving a fistful of glowsticks, and receives only a glancing blow. The girl shoves the bouncer and Hoyt reads *relax, baby* on her lips and *didn't think you'd catch me* on her body.

Scottie tugs at his elbow. "Let's go."

Hoyt doesn't quite understand how they teleport

from one club to the next. One minute he's stepping out into purple plumes of cigarette smoke, and then he's stepping up to a soaked bar, pressing his elbows into the watery surface. His tongue has grown so wide, so impossibly large, that he can hardly manage more than a mumbled order. The bartender, thick eyebrows kissing, asks him to repeat himself twice before Callum steps in. Hoyt staggers to the toilets and washes his hands so he has a reason to linger. The mirror shows a man; glassy-eyed, flushed, but with a perfectly normal-sized tongue. Maybe Gaz put something in his drink. He rubs a soapy, wet hand over his chin, and is surprised to feel sharp bristles already. A Killers song plays—something he knows, finally—and he howls the chorus all the way back to the dancefloor.

The supply of beer is infinite. He's a conveyor belt, built to imbibe. Grimsby and Jeremy are talking in a corner, heads close together, hands carefully far apart, and Hoyt wonders—not for the first time— whether they're screwing. Not that it matters. More girls for him. Pedro shepherds him outside, ignoring his complaints, ignoring the fact that he had a fifth of a pint left. "Scottie wants to leave," he shrugs.

Hoyt stumbles over the doorstep but Callum steadies him. Up close, his shirt is soaked under the arms and he smells like wet dog. A few meters away from the entrance of the third club, three girls are clustered together. One blonde sitting on the curb, legs akimbo. One shoe on, one off. Broken heel in her hand. One blonde kneeling, murmuring softly, stonewashed denim jacket at odds with her black jumpsuit and strappy shoes. A dark-haired girl standing, arms crossed, wearing a *this again, really* expression and a slinky, emerald dress that makes him think of pine forests and how long it's been since he went camping, like, proper camping, under the stars, away from all this light pollution. The pack approaches. Hoyt's not so drunk that he can't count. *Three of them. Seven of us.* He feels a momentary flicker of unease but so what? They're nice guys. They're not doing anything wrong. They fan out and form a natural semi-circle around the girls. Jeremy ducks into the nearby alley and the sound of water cascading follows a moment later.

"You okay?" Scottie addresses the standing girl.

"Yeah. Been a night." Irish accent lilting. *Nice eyes,* Hoyt thinks, dark as ...dark as... something. Dark as stout, maybe. She double-takes. "Thanks for asking, though."

Scottie smiles; it's not the smug smirk he normally uses, but a full five thousand lumens. "Need a pick me up? I've got a few left. From a reputable source, obviously."

The girls don't look at each other, but the blonde's denim-clad shoulders are rising towards her ears.

Green Girl drops her arms to her side. "What have you got?"

"Mish," the one on the ground says. "I want to go home."

She's still only got eyes for Scottie. "I don't have any money left."

"Maybe you could pay another way." Her eyebrow quirks but she isn't saying no. Maybe it's the extra shots Jeremy bought in the first club, maybe it's just a moment of overconfidence borne from a charmed life, but Scottie's eyes flick towards the other two and he adds, "Maybe you all could."

It's the first time Hoyt has seen Scottie misjudge a situation. Another girl, another street, another time, and that first line would kill. Probably has, considering how he delivered it. But the presence of the lads is too much, tipping the scale. One man is sexy. Two is manageable. Seven is dangerous. Maybe Scottie's never really been in a position where he hasn't been top dog, in control of the situation. Maybe he hasn't read the newspaper articles about the recent rash of attacks on women outside clubs—not that women outside clubs have ever had an easy time of it. Maybe he doesn't think the warnings should apply to him, as handsome and trustworthy as he evidently believes he is.

The girl in the emerald dress shifts, her heels scraping against the gritty pavement and Hoyt's buzz is harshing. A siren wail blasts, so close he flinches; all seven of the lads swivel at once to face the same direction. North-east. Funny, he doesn't see any flashing blue lights, but he feels as if he could pinpoint the exact street where the ambulance is. The exact house, even. When he looks back, the blonde is helping the sitting girl to her feet, and Green Girl looks freaked out. "What?" Her accent is even more pronounced.

"Didn't you hear that?" Gaz inches forward, offers an ingratiating smile that doesn't land.

"I didn't hear anything." Green Girl steps back, and the girl with the broken heel clutches at her upper arm. She's got goosebumps. They all have. Hoyt is reminded of his most-recent ex, the way her flesh pebbled under his fingers whenever he tried to ignite a flame. "I think we're going to call it a night, lads. Thanks so."

"Hey," Scottie says, holding out a hand. "Wait a second. You don't have to go."

"No, yeah, we're grand, yeah," she agrees, backing away. "Nice to meet you."

There's a moment when Hoyt feels the night bulge and split, like cells dividing. A moment when one set of lads shrugs, makes a few ribald jokes, moves on. But this isn't that night, and this isn't that road. Scottie, jaw working as if he's grinding down a thick, meaty bone between his molars, pursues the girls into the alley.

The pack follow.

The girls emerge at the other end, doused in scarlet light from a bright bar sign. They trot past the pub, past the two bouncers guarding a small cordoned-off smoking area. One of the bouncers glances over but the other is mid-punchline and then they're both laughing, distracted. Downhill, the girls pick up the pace on the winding street, heading towards the site of the old gallows and Scottie calls again, wolf-whistles, laughs when they ignore him. Hoyt winces. His hands are rubbery, hanging by his sides like newly-executed criminals.

The girls are speed-walking. Scottie begins to jog.

Hoyt blares a warning noise; something unintelligible. The pack ignores him. The girls turn a corner at the T junction and then reappear. The one in the emerald dress shouts something—a challenge, maybe, rather than a warning—and then it happens.

The woman with the red hair appears on the other side of the street and doesn't say a word. Doesn't entice with a cocked finger, doesn't raise an eyebrow. Just makes eye contact. It's plenty. They're turning before they even recognize her, something in their bones humming the oldest song in the world. She's stunning. Gorgeous wouldn't cover it. Ethereal, maybe. Foxy. Jeans so tight they look like they've been painted on. Black leather jacket, curving soft as butter. If she's wearing something underneath the jacket, Hoyt can't see any trace of it.

Scottie's lips part and Hoyt can read his mind. It's what they're all thinking; aye aye, here's a skirt worth chasing. The world glitters around the fox, soot-stained red brick shimmering like a portal to another world. Like a fantasy shot in soft focus, with too much Vaseline smeared on the lens. Maybe Gaz really did spike his drink.

The pack share a glance. There's an unspoken understanding. The one who catches her, gets her.

Tale as old as time.

She settles into her stride before Hoyt can even blink. Expensive trainers hit the pavement as they whoop and holler after her. Bugle calls, designed to unnerve her and to spur them on. They're hot on her heels down King's Stable Road but lose her as they come in sight of the car park, looming like a stone prison, and Hoyt feels a stab of relief that the hunt might be over before it started. No such luck. Yowling, Gaz sprints forwards; Callum takes up the call as they thunder down the terrace, down into the Lawnmarket. Pushing their way through map-clutching tourists and baby-faced students with close-cropped haircuts and Gen Z glasses. They sight the fox again on the Mound, lose her again on Princes Street. Follow her round the curve of the castle road—which doesn't make sense, Hoyt knows, since they should have been facing the opposite direction—until they emerge, winded but every fibre thrilling, on Lothian Road. She leads them through an empty underpass and along narrow backstreets, passing through less and less gentrified areas as they get farther from the city centre.

The alcohol in his system hasn't evaporated. He's still hammered. Bungalowed. Absolutely melted. And yet somehow he's not only keeping pace with the rest but almost drawing level with Scottie, who snaps a quick warning. Hoyt drops back fractionally, content to pick his moment.

Another lost scent as they race through Slateford, stone cottages passing in a blur. Pausing at a crossroad, Grimsby and Jeremy don't seem as interested as the rest; they tussle on the corner, trying to get the other in a headlock, tongues lolling like puppies. Grimsby snaps at Jeremy's neck, aiming for the scruff, and whines when he misses and gets a dead-arm punch for his trouble. Scottie's nose is high in the air— a tiny, pink mountain peak—and Hoyt can't remember if he's always looked this sleek, this feral. His eyes are black, the pupils blown to the size of dinner plates.

The breeze shifts. Trail caught. They're off again, running in a tight-knit pack. Lithe gym bodies stretching out, caught in flashes between the lampposts like amber-shaded polaroids. Silent now, intent on the quarry. Strange how quarry can mean both prey and a deep pit. A flash of red, scaling a fence in one fluid motion. She never looks back. Hoyt wonders if that's part of the game. Maybe its a rule—maybe if she looks back, she's lost; lost as Lot's wife, lost as Orpheus. Scottie hurdles the fence, long legs eating up the air. Hoyt leaps the fence one-handed, nails digging into the soft wood for purchase. Lavender rises on the night air. Manure. The curiously tart smell of potato peelings.

He's beginning to tire, now. They're almost at Sighthill and still she's keeping abreast of them. Scottie strains forward, t-shirt soaked, face pushed into the night like he's nuzzling a lover. Hoyt refuses to give up. Scottie could have any girl he wants, any time. Why should he have this one, too?

The fox makes it to the lit tunnel—single halogen bulb pulsing like a half-hard cock—and through the other side. The lads clatter through after her, emerge braying on the other side. Milling about in confusion, heads tilted to catch the slightest whisper on the wind, glancing back down the flickering tunnel as if they're waiting for a jump-scare. Hoyt leans against the entrance, opens his mouth and drinks the moon. Feels it soothe his burning throat; slide cold, thick, and white, down into his gut.

Scottie growls. A low, impatient burr. They're standing in the middle of a small paved area, just below the bypass, but Hoyt hasn't seen or heard a car since they left the city centre. There's four entrances to this area; two heading back towards town, one pointing away. The pack wait until Scottie picks one and starts jogging towards it. They follow automatically but he spins, snarling, protecting what's his. They understand. *All's fair, and all that.* They're on their own now. Callum and Pedro split off, heading for one tunnel, and Gaz picks the third. Grimsby and Jeremy are staring into each other's eyes. No one is paying attention to Hoyt, who eases around and pads after Scottie. Hesitates. Retreats. Heads back down the tunnel the way they came. Emerging from the tunnel, blinking the sticky residue of the light away, he's somehow unsurprised to see the fox poised. Waiting for him.

Up close, she's more accessible. Less movie-star, more girl-next-door. Still bangable, though. He subsides, panting, and make a bit of a show of checking the tunnel. They've all gone. "Sorry about that. Don't worry, you're safe now. I wouldn't let them hurt you." He's not sure that's true, but it doesn't matter.

She tilts her head. Smiles with all her teeth. He approaches, pantomimes open palms. Leans in, leans down, but she pulls away. Rage surges and that old song hums in his bones, speaks to him of unspoken promises. Drums up ancient, corybantic resentments. "I could call them back. You can't outrun us forever." Vulpine eyes follow the movement of his lips. His throat is dry and tight. New fur pushes against his collar. "Anyway, don't I deserve a reward? You led me on a fair chase."

He means to flirt, but the panting makes his voice rougher. She retreats another pace, into the sparse trees. He steps forwards again, into her personal space, and reaches for her waist. She slides through his fingers.

"Bitch," he seethes, grabbing fistfuls of air.

He swings for her; not a real punch, but it wouldn't have to be. Just a closed fist clubbing her temple would put her down for ten. That's all he'd need. He misses. Lashes out again. Misses again. Smashes his knuckles on the rough bark. She's everywhere and nowhere. In his nostrils, deep in his pockets, evading his touch. He goes for a bear hug, for a clinch. Tries to pin her down but it's impossible, like trying to nail his own breath to the wall.

He blinks and he's alone. The enormity of his actions pours over him in one breathless tsunami. He chokes down a half-sob, then punches his own chest, his jaw, anywhere he can reach. He's as bad as the rest. Maybe worse.

She's vanished. The night chugs him down in one gulp, chases him with the aroma of manhood: hops and regret, sweat and shame, Gaultier and denial.

MISSED CONNECTIONS

Missed Connection

You were battling for control of your father's throne, with only a single tooth from the lost king to prove your parentage. I was the assistant to the gardener who provided the herbs required for your wizard to perform the ancestry spell. When the crown was finally placed on your head, your brother's corpse lying twisted in a puddle of blood at your feet, our eyes met. Something sprouted inside me—something I'd never felt before. Those fresh roses on your breakfast table were my speciality, by the way. If you'd like to find out what else on my body is green, come see our arboretum sometime.

Connection Correction

To the now-queen, I would like to clarify that I wasn't actually suggesting I had a fungus somewhere upon my person. The green thing was a play on words (perhaps you've never heard the term 'green thumb'? Totally understandable, your education was likely focused more on geopolitical strategy than gardening) but I see now how it could have been misread as disease. I know you've been busy fending off assassins sent by your cousin, who seems a bit miffed about the whole kin-slaying thing, but the offer of a romantic evening still stands. My shed has a very solid, lockable door.

Correction to the Correction

To the Queen of the Still Grasses, the Unquenchable Fires, and the whole general Askiian Realm—I am dictating this from your dungeon. The nightguard was kind enough to help me out once I'd explained the misunderstanding. I'm sure we'll laugh about this some day! In hindsight, yes, that last message did sound a bit kidnappy, or at least non-consensual, which wasn't my intention at all. Look, I'll admit I'm not very good at wooing. I've never been a knight or a courtier. I'm just a gardener; I'm good at trees. I'm good at bushes. I'd happily show you how good I am at bushes.

Sad Chidings and Congratulations

Your Majesty, there was really no need to arrest Deek. He's a good soul who believes in the power of romantic love, and pardon me but it seems a little unkind to chain him up next to me. I'm sure that's not really the impression you want to give your subjects, is it? Oh and congratulations on defeating those assassins. I hear you've made a beautiful display of their severed heads outside the castle walls. I'd love to see them but, as you know, I'm still locked in the dungeon.

Confession

Your Majesty, this is a very difficult message to write. The thing is, Deek and I got to talking—you wouldn't believe how much spare time we have down here—and it turns out we're really quite similar. I must confess, that after much consideration, I have to dismiss what you and I experienced those many months ago as a mere flash of lust. After all, we'd never chatted, never got to really know each other, while Deek and I have developed a deeper bond, supported each other through various tortures (your men are really quite enthusiastic, aren't they?) and as such, something truly magical has bloomed. It's early days yet, but I dare to hope that such an honest and tender connection may last.

Conclusion and Conciliations

To the Queen of the Still Grasses, the Unquenchable Fires, the Askiian Realm, the Cill Mountains, the Morrow Lands, and the Obsidian Mines—gosh, you have been busy! Well done on the expansion plans. I must thank you for finally releasing Deek and I from the dungeon. While I can't say I enjoyed my stay there much, without it I would never have met the love of my life. Please keep an eye out for your invitation to our wedding, which should arrive shortly. Would love to see you there!

ON THE WING

When he wakes up, it's to the smell of hot, clean cotton. His wife is already ironing his white shirt, choosing a tie based on the pattern of the clouds which scud past the window. She's a glean of herons, long-legged under an oyster-pale silk slip. Slippery and pliant.

When she makes breakfast, her husband scrolls through the day's headlines and spoons runny egg into his mouth. As a kid, he'd thought that fried eggs looked like vulnerable suns; as an adult he knows better. This shade of orange, tiger-bright, would indicate that the sun was dying, which wouldn't suit his plans at all. He's a realm of kingfishers, flashing blue blazes—the hottest colour a flame can be.

When he checks his phone, he frowns at the screen. For another man, a frown might herald a coming storm. With her husband, she knows, it's simply the way he reacts to all news, whether good or bad. He's a parcel of penguins; black and white and stoic all over.

When she leans over him to pour more coffee, he swipes the message away, but not before she glimpses the contents. A body—nude—neither his nor hers. A clamor of rooks clanging inside the vast timpani of her chest, echoing rounded copper notes. She turns the tap on, soaps the dishes. The washing-up liquid is not clean and sharp, like lemon, but rather a frothing apple-scent, concave, like a smell collapsed.

When he performs his ablutions, he's a drum of goldfinches; scrubbing the bristles against his teeth in time with a familiar melody in his mind, washing his face and patting it down with a musky, pine-needle aftershave more suited to the wolf than the woodcutter. She kneels on the hardwood hallway floor and buffs his brogues to a brilliant shine until she can see the pale oval of her own face.

When she hears the smack and flick of his towel against the bathroom tiles, mere feet from the laundry basket, she's a quarrel of sparrows—a thousand-fold origami flock, each a darting, stinging papercut. When she walks into the bedroom he's dressing and belting, buttoning collar and cuff. She pools the words, gathers them together like goslings under the trembling wing of her tongue; he kisses her on the cheek and exits the house, whistling, neither noticing nor caring.

When he swerves onto the motorway with practiced ease, he's a pride of peacocks. Switching the radio to a popular channel, he drums the steering wheel to the beat and chimes in at the chorus to a song last sung while nine-pints-sunk. The house he left behind is a silent sentence, punctuated by the full-stop smashing of crockery, the commas of curses, the semi-colons of sobbing.

When she packs her suitcase, she takes only what she needs. Layering neon t-shirts on top of pajamas too modest to please him; a bright lasagna of her own style. She's an unkindness of ravens, pouring a full jar of honey into his sock drawer. Spraying shaving cream into his closet, graffiting her name in bursts of citrus foam.

When he waits in line for a free coffee from the company-owned machine, he hits the button twice. Strutting down the hallway, he's a prattle of parrots, exchanging jokes with the janitor, ribbing the guys in accounts about the latest football score. Holding both plastic cups aloft; common libations to double-faced gods.

When she locks the front door behind her, the key is stiff and unyielding. For a moment she wonders whether to retreat inside, to unpack her bag, to hibernate for a season or two of denial. A single caw sounds from above. She counts the birds perched on the gutter pipe, doffs an imaginary cap like her grandfather used to do. She's a gulp of magpies; one for sorrow, two for joy.

When he stops at the front desk to chat with his mistress, he slides one coffee over with a smile and keeps the twin. She answers a phone, holds up a finger to indicate that she'll be right with him. He's a charm of hummingbirds, hovering steadily. The thrum of his desire is almost too low to hear, like whalesong—mournful, ribbed, fathomed. Still, the mistress is attuned to the crackle and hiss of his frequency by now.

When the woman who was once his wife turns the key in the ignition, she feels the rumble start in front of her knees and wriggle down, until the car is purring under the soles of her boots. Flushed, blistered, she's a ruby of robins. Rubies, after all, are the gemstone of home and hearth. These things were important, once upon a time. She'd left the ring on the front doorstep—right in the middle, so the man who was once her husband can't miss it like he misses everything else. The expensive jewel fizzles in the sunlight. Colour, clarity, carat, cut—the four qualities men look for in a rock and a woman.

When he texts the woman who was once his wife to tell her he'll be home late, her silence doesn't alarm him. He's already busy making plans, fortifying his defenses, loading lies like crossbow bolts, each capable of slamming through the sternest defenses. He's a pitying of doves, clustered snug and peacefully in the driver's seat of his car, watching his mistress unbutton her blouse, her skin coated with the last gasps of a brilliant, bloody sunset.

When she turns the radio on, miles later, it asks her *hey what's going on*, it asks *what have you done for me lately*, it asks *have you ever seen the rain*, and she drives out of town and the sky is new-wound-pink with not a single cloud in sight and above the road a single black dot hovers above an open field, hovers, hovers. Flaps once. Plummets. Rises again with nothing in its open beak, not even a question, and she thinks that's how she'd like to be from now on—not a kettle of hawks, but a tower of falcons. Unlimbed. Torched. Rebuilt.

DRAWBACK

(published in Et Sequitur)

he bench in the gallery looks comfortable—padded with plush velvet—but the girl's parents don't approve of lingering, especially in places like this. The walls are a deep, comforting garnet, like being tucked inside your mother's cheek, squirrel-close; like being blown, dandelion feather-light, on the hearty strength of your father's yawn. The family examine each artwork for a similar period of time—frequently a question is asked and answered on both sides—before they move on at a relentless, glacial pace. The girl makes notes in a small journal that her parents purchased beforehand at a supermarket, probably to stop her asking for one at the gift shop. Her pencil is imprinted with the name of the bank where her father works. "Memories are our own creations," he reminds her. "It's up to us to record and maintain them."

They finally pause at the painting the girl has wanted to study since she walked in, which contains four figures in total. Under a stormy sky, three are huddled together under a green umbrella. One is running away, receding into the distance, holding a newspaper over its head. A dark smudge to the left of the running figure, close to the ground, might be a dog. The background is lined with trees and the umbral, splotchy suggestion of flowers.

The nurse spends her days washing and feeding elderly patients, checking their medications, updating charts. She witnesses the ebb and flow of memories, which move like a tide; on good days, they wash over the shoreline of consciousness, bathing everything in bright lights. Gilded edges form around each mental snapshot: a grandchild dressed up for Halloween, a Christmas dinner with all the family, births and celebrations dribbling with champagne and confetti. Sweet smells, savoury sights. Each memory a filling, nutritious meal.

On bad days, seaweed soaks up thought into salted strands, strangles her patients with paranoia and the lingering taste of shadows; no matter how long bottled up, fear never ceases to be potent, as bitter as a lightning flash. Insecurities and jealousies—in dappled forest shades of lichen and bark—splinter under the weight of thought. If a tree falls in the forest, the nurse wonders, why can't it bear witness to its own destruction?

When these memories recede like a tide, her patients' minds are left barren and bare, punctuated only with the occasional treasured shell. Conversations—like footprints—linger but do not last, and yet—

The umbrella in the painting is a sharp, fresh green, like a rose stem snipped in its prime. The girl thinks the figures beneath must be a family, with their stiff backs and same, straw-colored hair and the way they all lean together but don't touch, painted careful millimetres apart for all eternity. When she looks up, her mother's face in profile is thorny, as beautiful as an iceberg. It is impossible to tell whether or not her mother approves of the painting, and the girl feels panic splinter into shards, poking the inside of her ribs. She raises the pen and touches the nib to the paper, but does not write.

"Well? What do you think?" Her father's hand, hot and heavy on her shoulder, burns like an eclipsed sun.

—there is nothing. Faces aren't quite as clear as they once were. Photographs gripped tight in wrinkled fingers. Nothing. Voices, echoing through time, of the dead and maybe-dead, who can still be heard between the crackle of record grooves, and clipped accents on the wireless and—

Nothing. And then sometimes, something, on the tip of

their tongues. A hand raised to brush back hair that no longer frizzes or billows in the breeze, or perhaps to greet a long-lost friend, momentarily obscured by a crowd. Swallowed up. Or down, as the case may be.

The nurse takes their hands, listens to their stories. Coaxes them into washing, eating, doing a little seated exercise. Their eyes stumble after her like newborn lambs. Faces like elderly moons, always rotating to face her, to watch what she is doing as she moves around the room, making notes, tidying up, checking medication levels. Cholinesterase inhibitors—donepezil, rivastigmine, galantamine.

The umbrella was teal, the girl thinks. It's been over a year since the family last visited a museum, and over three years since they visited the gallery with the umbrella painting. Occasionally, her parents fight but more often they're distant; orbiting ellipses that only connect twice a year, out of sync. She often wonders about this particular gallery—at the time, she'd been anxious to say the right thing, to record the right memories, but now she recalls the moment as a time when things were perfect. Frozen. *Movement is the enemy of beauty*, she thinks. *Growth is ugly.* She asks if they can return to the gallery but her parents put the idea off, week by week, until it becomes clear they have no intention of indulging the request. They exist in time like sharks, always gliding forwards, never repeating an experience. The girl satisfies herself with memories; both written and mental, but gaps trouble her.

Her father's hand on her shoulder, warm and reassuring. Her mother's usually perfect eyeliner, slightly smudged. Something had happened that morning—a telephone call, perhaps, radiating staccato murmurs, foreshadowing death. A blister on her toe, not yet born but gestating with raw potential.

The nurse knows when an end is near. She watched a documentary on tsunamis once; if the first part of a tsunami to reach the coast is a trough, rather than a wave crest, then the water along the shoreline is hauled back, as if the ocean is taking a deep breath, ready to scream. Parts of the shoreline which would normally be underwater— protected, invisible, subconscious—are exposed. The narrator called it a drawback, but the nurse can't see anything wrong with a cautionary sign about the future. Forewarned, as they say, is forearmed.

Often, patients talk of love and loss; a miscarriage, a divorce, the one that got away. She's heard the rattle of every skeleton, no matter how long they've been locked up or how deeply. The tsunami pulls back the curtain, allows her to see the actors mouthing their words, the stagehands moving to and fro. It's not her place to judge—she, who has never married, whose affairs have been perfunctory. She sandwiches her patients' cold hands between the warmth of her own, and reassures them that whatever happens, she will be present. No one will die alone. The final moments of a tree will always be seen and heard.

The umbrella in the painting was turquoise; a brilliant, pure peal, resounding like a church bell. In her thirties, growth is no longer ugly but a joyful necessity. The girl is now a woman, a medical professional, a chronic journaller. She recalls her father's hand on her shoulder, as light as a question. The interrobang of her mother's perfume was a thin mist of fragrance, green-leaf-volatile as cut grass, lacking the baritone of earth-rich foundational notes; a balloon, let go on purpose, sailing into a blue sky.

The blister, somewhere on her foot, is no longer anchored to any particular part. A loose bandage, covering a deeper, yawning ache. Her parents are echoes, fading in time. She has never been a parent herself, has shied away from the idea of raising a new human from acorn to oak. Perhaps she is not good at beginnings, but she understands instinctively what a proper ending should be.

The nurse has tasted loneliness, drunk it like an aged wine, and found it pleasing. The patients are her children—older than she is by decades, birthed on death's door, knocking, pulling back the brass hammer, inviting themselves inside. Life is an umbrella, she believes, a temporary shelter from the downpour of crises. To stand under the arc, to be at one with the curve—dry, intact—is a gift she intends to share for as long as she owns it.

The umbrella was blue; a shiny, glossy cobalt, regal in its richness. In her fifties, her joints have begun to creak. In cold weather her left wrist, once broken, aches to foretell a storm. She recalls her father's hand hovering over her shoulder, exerting no pressure; after all, an experienced rider has no need to use the reins, only his knees. The smell of her mother's perfume, no longer a cloud but a sparse connection of atoms; no longer able to be smelled as one complete scent, like trying to read an entire word from letters hidden on different continents of a globe. Even records can change under scrutiny; she believes the universe can be knowable or locatable—not both. Late into the night, at the bedside of an old man wheezing his last breaths, she reads aloud from yellowed notebooks scrawled in a childish hand.

The old man sometimes asks who she is; the woman does not know how to answer. Later, when his heart has stilled and her tears have wetted the paper, adding another layer to the memory—written then, accessed now, lived countless times—the sound of a dog barking outside, rain drumming on her window, stirs something long buried under settled dust and she wakes up—

—*in this bed, as this woman. Her hands and feet are cold but the window is closed, and yet when she blinks the window is open, blinks again and it's closed and the calendar on the wall reads the previous month. The picture has changed too.*

Perhaps it does not matter what colour the umbrella is, only that there was an umbrella and now she steps out from under it, unshielded, untangled. She is a girl—was a nurse—is a woman—was a memory.

The umbrella is blue; the brightest, primary blue. The rest of the memory is stillwater, reduced to grey, as if boiled too long. The tsunami crests—

crests, crests,

and hangs there, *waiting,*

waiting, *waiting,*

for the right time to fall.

CAKE BY THE OCEAN

(published in The Razor)

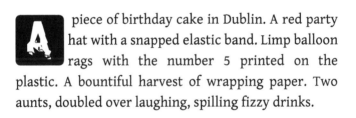 piece of birthday cake in Dublin. A red party hat with a snapped elastic band. Limp balloon rags with the number 5 printed on the plastic. A bountiful harvest of wrapping paper. Two aunts, doubled over laughing, spilling fizzy drinks.

A raspberry sorbet in Majorca. Chapped lips. Heat shimmers on wavy pavements. Thick smears of suntan lotion. A late curfew. A boy who smelled like the liquid mixture used to blow bubbles. The first grains of sexuality, trickling downwards.

A torn hunk of Victoria Sponge on Blackpool beach,

following too-hot chips and tomato ketchup. Windblown hair. Seagulls squalling, syncopated, over tinny fairground music. A group of teen friends already growing apart.

Something chocolatey and unpronounceable in Normandy. Someone else's headphones, thudding like twin hearts. A girl with a thin eyebrow scar. A long train ride to an unfamiliar, warm bed. A promise quickly broken.

A cronut in New York. Vaped cotton candy breath. Ice clinking against a frosted glass. Knee-bones kissing under a small table. A connection spanning distance and time. Familiar, green-needle perfume. Nervous-eyed newscasters reading headlines with placid lips.

Two frosted vanilla cupcakes in Shannon. A text received; *Babe I miss you already*. Fights in the bus depot. Broken glass underfoot, crunchy and pale as January frost. Streaks of dried brown blood on the linoleum floor. A text received; *I'm scared stay safe I'm so scared I wish you hadn't left I don't know what I'm gonna do okay always remember that I love you I love you always forever I swear I love I love*

Spiced gingerbread in Dublin city centre. Abandoned cars. Empty streets. A hammer hooked into a belt loop, just in case. A lack of cell phone signal. The weasel-bite of panic, nipping constantly.

Black forest gateaux in a seaside cafe. Shop doors, as wide open as coughing mouths. Occasional twisted bodies, scuttling like crabs. No broadcasts on any TV or radio channels. A light, drizzling rain. A reason to use the hammer, twice.

Two mouldy shortbread fingers on a ferry. A crumpled map. A badly-bandaged wound, leaking relief. Calm green ocean on all sides. A pod of dolphins, competing for most spectacular jump. A smile—almost.

Stale scones in the Scottish highlands. Fresh milk. A herd of deer, more curious than afraid. Loneliness, thicker than the down-feather winter coat in the closet. A farmer's gun. Plenty of time to practice. Nothing left but memories.

JUNE 323 BCE

(published by Flash Fiction Online)

If I had to choose, I'd say I'm Luxembourg; small, neat, boxy. Luxembourg's capital city is also called Luxembourg. Sometimes I think about my brain and how, if the brain is the capital city of the body, my brain must also be called Harrison. The heart is different. I don't know if my heart is called Harrison. Maybe the heart is like the second-largest capital city, like Glasgow or Marseille—I don't know what that makes the liver, because they're usually heavier than the brain, and no one has been able to tell me yet what the correct corresponding entity should be.

David would be Alexandria. He says that's his

favourite place name in the whole world.

After school, I set out to find him. I start in Cyprus —the lowest branch of the big tree in the Delaney's front garden—and then I cruise across the sea of asphalt, arms open wide like a condor, until I alight on the beaches of Egypt.

When I get to the crossroads near the church, I press the button and wait even though there's no traffic. Today, David comes from the south, and his left cheek is swollen. "We were in Asmara this morning," he says. "At the dentist."

"Capital of Eritrea," I say, and he tosses me a lemon drop from his pocket.

"Not bad."

"Maybe if you didn't carry so many lemon drops you wouldn't need to go to Asmara."

"Did you know that the old man who used to live in your house carried strawberry bonbons around all the time?" He shoves a hand into the pocket, wiggles it to make the wrappers crinkle. "I prefer citrus." His left eye has bloomed a ferocious purple. "Sour. Tart."

"Acetic. Bitter. Piquant." He throws me another. I can't help staring. "What's wrong with your tooth?"

There hadn't been anything wrong with his mouth at school yesterday. Or his eye. In our last class of the day, he'd answered all the questions Mr Kipphut had asked. Answered everything correctly until Sam and Budd had started mimicking him in a shrill, piggy voice. Then he'd stopped answering, even when Mr

Kipphut made them hush.

"Did I ever tell you," David leans closer, "that the dentist's assistant has a smile as wide as the Ganges?"

I don't say anything. His story doesn't make sense. My aunt works at the dentist's office and it's much further west, like Khartoum. My aunt says you can't always believe what people tell you, especially about their teeth.

"What, you don't think I could charm an older woman?" He smiles, then grimaces and touches a tentative finger to his cheek.

"Why did Budd tell you yesterday that pigs can't sweat?"

He pretends he's just spotted his lace is loose and kneels to fix it, but I can see him struggle to tug the knot out.

"Pigs use mud to cool down instead of sweat. I like pigs." I say. "Did you know that they're even-toed ungulates?"

He sighs, his face hidden. "Yes, Harrison, I did know that." He stands. "Want to go for a walk?"

"Which direction?"

He revolves, finger held out. "West."

David listens to me talking all the way to the park, then he takes the left swing because he knows I like the right one. A friend for life is the best kind, my mother says. I don't have many friends, so it's good to know he'll always be around. The chains rattle as I grip them above my head.

"Why is Alexandria your favourite?"

"You know why."

"I like to hear you tell it." I wait, poking wood chips with one sneaker.

"Alexander was the greatest." His voice slows, takes on a dreamy quality. "He assumed the throne after his father died. He sacked Thebes the following year before starting on Persia. He never faltered, never wavered." He breaks off. Budd, wearing a bleached t-shirt and cut off shorts, is ambling toward the park, cell phone held in front of his mouth. He's seen us; he's smiling but I don't think it's because he's happy.

David stands up so I do too. "Alexander cried because there were no more worlds left to conquer. Isn't that something?" He isn't smiling.

My stomach cramps because I've wanted to bring this up for weeks, ever since I found out the truth, but I didn't know how. I'm not good at guessing what the right time is. I'm not good at guessing what people are thinking. There's so much I'm not good at, like lying. "He never actually said that."

"Huh?"

"There's no proof. Catherine of Aragorn asked for a copy of Plutarch's Moralia in 1527, and the guy who made it for her included the real quote. If Alexander ever said such a thing," I pause but he doesn't say anything. His mouth is slightly open, and his eyebrows are raised. My father says that means surprise or shock or awe. I continue, "then probably what he actually said was the opposite. Something like 'can you believe there are infinite worlds, and I have not even conquered one?'"

David's looking at me as though he's never seen me before. I study his body language. Loose arms, feet pointing north, eyebrows now arching downwards.

"Are you mad at me? I can't tell."

He whistles, long and slow. "Well I'll be damned, Harrison. That's some good advice."

"It is?"

Budd kicks the gate. It rebounds off the metal fence. Reverberating. Rumbling. David doesn't flinch. "Hold out your hands."

Obediently, I comply. He pours the contents of his pocket into my waiting palms. A lemon-drop libation to his hero. I close my fingers over the crinkling wrappers.

"Keep these safe. Be my Hephaestion."

Budd stands at the open gate, oinking. He hasn't come in. He's waiting like a matador, knowing that the bull is going to have to come out sooner or later. David walks towards him as I unwrap a lemon drop. The sweetness invades my tongue like an onslaught of Macedonians.

THE ONE WHERE PARADISE BEGINS TO CRACK

The One With The Jam

He is a cruelly handsome man, with eyes like Brad Pitt and a mouth like a massacre. She is a cruelly beautiful woman, with hair like Sofia Vergara and eyes like late-stage syphilis. We stand together in the middle of Waitrose and study the rows of jellies, marmalades, and spreads as if they are a long-lost yet decipherable language.

"Don't forget the shopping list, darling," Emelie says, rooting around in her purse for her loyalty card. "We're out of lube, too."

The One Where Monica and Richard Are Just Friends

Ken winks at me and strolls around the corner, presumably to fetch some from the health and beauty aisle. I carry the empty wire basket and trail after Emelie as she frets about precisely how chunky each of the chutneys might be. "After all," she says, "the cheese to cracker to condiment ratio has to be relatively—I mean, mathematically speaking, it's really quite—"

She stops as a satyr pushes a trolley into our aisle. A curly-haired baby sits in the little built-in seat of the trolley and kicks her tiny hooves against the metal bars. The satyr locks eyes with Emelie; the trolley screeches to a halt so fast I expected to see tyre burn on the recently-mopped floor. He lifts four fingers from his grip on the trolley's handle and waves, reluctantly.

"Oh, hi." Emelie steps forwards. I can smell her discomfort, steaming into the air like warm apple pie. "How've you been, Calzentay?"

The satyr rubs his right horn, and opens his mouth. A blast of hot wind, tasting of creosote and summer evenings, blows my feathers backward. "Totally," Emelie agrees, smiling; her eyes are crinkled, not the way they do when she looks at Ken and I, but different, less acute angles.

I nod politely. It's been a tough week—all I've been able to utter are catchphrases from *Frasier* and I don't really think any of them are a particularly suitable way to greet one's current partners' ex-lovers.

The One Where Ross And Rachel Take A Break

The baby stretches a hand out, tiny fingertips brushing the surface of the jars on the shelves. The satyr blows a dandelion-soft breath towards her, eyes gleaming with adoration. When he turns back to us, his shoulders straighten, and the wind which leaves his mouth is a crispy autumn breeze, with just the faintest suggestions of bonfires in the distance.

"Yeah, totally. Nice to see you too," Emelie watches him roll past.

"Tossed salad and scrambled eggs!" I announce, and wrap my wing around her.

"I'm fine." She sighs. "It just ended rather badly, I'm afraid. Too many hurt feelings all round. Things said in the heat of the moment."

"Goodnight, Seattle."

"No, nothing to do with children. We do want them, eventually. But Calzentay wasn't ..." she searches for the words, eyes skimming over the jam labels. "I don't know. He just wasn't keen on—"

Ken appears before she can finish her thought.

The One With The East German Laundry Detergent

"Hey, was that—" he asks.

"Yes." Emelie steps away from me and fidgets with a belt loop on her jeans.

An indecipherable look passes between them. A moment lingers; longer than heartbeat, shorter than a held breath.

"It's as if you'd forgotten that not three days ago, I was punched in the face by a man now dead," I remind them, holding up my empty basket.

Ken drops the bottle of lube into the basket, then stretches up and kisses my cheek. "Of course, sweetheart. It's adorable how much you love brunch."

I flap my wings in a rough approximation of a human shrug. Who doesn't love brunch?

The One With The Apothecary Table

Back in their flat, we cut cheese into thin circles and chunky cubes. We halve ripe vine tomatoes and drop them, weeping, into a bowl of dark, trembling leaves. We shred basil. We sprinkle croutons. We slice cold meats and spicy sausages. We crack the hard crust of a fresh tiger loaf and saw off thick wedges of soft bread, big as doorstoppers. We core apples and segment oranges and deseed pomegranates and pare pears, unwinding their skins until their sweet flesh is exposed, grainy and moist, to the still air. We lay everything on the dining room table, which bears the weight heroically like Atlas, holding up the world on slender wooden struts. I stroke the table with a single claw, careful not to scratch the finish.

"Don't worry, it's only IKEA," Ken says, apologetically.

"I am *wounded!*" I squawk dramatically, clutching my chest, and he laughs.

"You're right, nothing to be ashamed of in this day and age." He selects a bottle from the well-stocked sideboard. "My father always says the chairs he buys there last longer than the ones his neighbour gets from the fancy furniture shop on the high street. I'm not sure what he's doing to really test the longevity of a chair, though, and I'm not really keen to find out."

I perch on the special bench they bought for me, my claws gripping the thick wood, while he pours a dash of aniseed liquor into three smoked-glass shot glasses.

The One Where Heckles Dies

"There's a documentary about volcanoes playing at the indie cinema this afternoon," Emelie says, spreading chutney on a cracker. "Do you fancy coming with us?"

I nod. "Go ahead, caller, I'm listening."

"Who directed it?" Ken wants to know.

"I can't remember her name. The one who did that other film you liked, about rivers of molten electronics in Asia."

"I wouldn't say I enjoyed it, exactly," Ken corrects. "It was culturally significant. There's a difference."

She adds three cubes of cheese to her cracker. Considers. Takes one off and puts it on her plate. Bites into the remainder.

"Doctor Crane." I indicate that I'd like some of the salad.

Outside, a dog barks. A passing car thrums past the window and a flash of light, glinting from the windshield, momentarily blinds me. When the gleam fades from my eyes, nothing has changed in the room but my heart sinks. The feast which had once seemed bountiful and beautiful now lies ravaged, scavenged. I remind myself that I was part of this plunder, and that my feelings are simply part of my species' natural desire to replenish what we take from the landscape.

The One With Monica's Thunder

When our bellies are satiated, Ken piles dishes into his arms and wanders into the kitchen, where the sound of running water is accompanied by the asthmatic wheeze of the washing-up liquid bottle. Emelie gathers the remaining plates and I follow, watching as she carefully packs the leftovers into tupperware. Such a sweet habit—to preserve, to store, to protect. I wonder, not for the first time, what they'd look like holding one of my hatchlings; whether they want children who look like them, talk like them, think like them. I wonder if the changes wrought upon my body with the shifting of the seasons can be overcome by sheer willpower, if not love. I wonder if I want that, or if I simply feel an urge, sometimes, to see whether it is possible to defy my own desires and live unchecked.

Placing the last dish on the draining board, Ken dries his soapy hands and checks his watch. "We've still got an hour before the film starts, you know."

Emelie turns to me, smiling, and I shuffle forwards, careful not to bang my head again on their trendy, low-slung spotlight bar.

"Dear God, Niles," I murmur, as I bend, once more, to nuzzle their faces.

UPPER BOUT

(published by Flash Fiction Online)

The violin had curves like his mother. Electric guitars hung from wires as if dropped by angels, while trumpets blasted from all four corners of the display window. In pride of place, a glossy red drum kit crouched, motionless, like a heart waiting to beat. Struan pressed his hand-knitted, lumpy mittens to the icy glass, drinking in the view. The wind slid frosty fingers under his thin clothes—a threadbare Ramones t-shirt which had once belonged to his da, and charity shop jeans, neither thick enough to stave off the chilled air—while his little brother swung a scuffed and torn backpack around in a circle, eyes on the darkening heavens, ignoring the loud tuts of passersby who were forced to step into the road to avoid an accidental belting.

Everything in the shop window was out of reach; the black flute with the white tip, bursting from the left like an unlit firework. The fanned-out, pristine music books—not a single dog-ear or crumpled cover among the lot. Individually, he coveted each beautiful instrument, but what he desired most of all was to hear them join together in harmony. Cooperation towards a single perfect goal was an unattainable concept at home, but in an orchestra, amidst the gleaming music stands and the soft hush of turned pages, fusion would be a palpable thing. Incontrovertible proof that unity and stability existed, somewhere.

He stayed as long as he dared before Declan, bored of the familiar display, hammered the pedestrian button at the traffic lights. Hatless, they walked home; Rudolph noses glowing, cheap trainers sticking to rimy pavements. Ma cut up a single Granny Smith in rough strokes without taking her eyes off the soaps on the television. The knife slipped a couple of times. Flecks of blood spattered Struan's apple slices, but he ate them anyway because if he said anything, she was likely to shift the entire lot into the bin or hand them over to Declan, who would eat off the floor in a mineshaft without complaint. Besides, a conductor was like silent glue, holding the orchestra together. Never complaining, never causing any fissures or ripples, smoothing the passage from one brassy instrument to the next.

Da was on the nightshift again, so they had to sit quietly and do their homework. Even the TV was down as low as possible; the subtitles were on, even though Ma didn't like to read. When Da finally emerged from the bedroom, a waft of hot, greasy sleep billowing from his open robe, Ma got up from her armchair. In the hallway, his parents sidled past each other like undecided rams; chins down, heads tilted, weighing up the odds of injury. Sometimes fights ended in rutting, but more often than not, someone bled. He craned through the open door and chirped a greeting, deflecting attention onto himself, and breathed a sigh when his parents passed into different rooms.

Declan kicked at invisible enemies, making the couch jiggle, and whined about missing his cartoons. Struan passed over the remote and slid off the sticky leather, snuck past the doorway leading into the kitchen, where Da sliced the heads off fish and tossed them into the sink. A callous executioner. A big pot of peeled potatoes were boiling—it smelled better than the eye-watering stench of the fryer. Chips often came out too-skinny and too-tanned, like the teen dragons who guarded the salon on the high street. Long, turquoise claws, to match their painted eyelids.

He crept along the hallway, fingers strumming the wall, until he reached his tiny bedroom. Little more than a cupboard, really, but he'd crammed it full of invisible music; soft skeins of clarinet solos, swinging from hole to hole in the patchwork ceiling. Plastic building blocks of double bass notes piled high on the flaking windowsill. Liquid glass pooling in a chipped mug, poured sparingly by a harp duo in long glissandos. He sprawled out on the bare mattress, hands conducting in sharp, defined strokes.

Brass coming in here, strings rising just so. Percussion to the right. The space around him contracted into a single portal, shimmering like a blown bubble. Beyond, a wide wooden stage, whispering his name. Struan stepped through onto the boards without hesitation, rolled his shoulders. His old clothes were gone; now he was swathed in a black suit and a white shirt, gleaming brighter than anything his ma had ever bleached. The captive audience of fish heads stared up at him, bug-eyed and awestruck. A baton in his hand, sturdy and powerful, as if it had always been there.

The music rose around him, painting the air in colour. A yellow C, repeated twice, followed by a minor chord in burgundy. A thin pink melody swelled through the cerulean fog. One deep breath. Through the portal, his name resounded; a bass note, wrapped in salted steam. His cheeks were wet; his small chest heaved with the effort of keeping the desire contained, of keeping reality at bay. A building crescendo waxed, soaring high above his head, into the rafters and through the terracotta tiles of the theatre. Final notes fluttered down like plucked feathers. His lungs ripened in rose petals, drowned in cloaks. Fish heads cheered wildly, applause bleeding from invisible fins. He held the baton high to extend the last exquisite moment before the lights blinked out.

One day the orchestra would be in his hands and not just his head. *An artist without a canvas*, his music teacher had promised, *is no less of an artist.*

YOUNGBLOOD

ive days after his untimely death, Rob stood outside my house, staring up at the window of my first-floor bedroom.

Every few seconds, a low, guttural snarl leaked out over bloodless lips. His skinny arms spasmed, hands hanging loosely at his sides. He made no attempt to move a few feet to his right where the latched gate would have allowed him easy access to the paved garden pathway, lined with rose bushes planted during the Clinton years.

"I think it's romantic, really." Yvette tapped the window with one long, scarlet nail. "Kinda sweet, know what I mean?"

"It doesn't feel romantic. It feels like he's

committing a crime right now."

"He's dead, Suzanne," my sister said, as if explaining basic manners to a child. "He's not exactly thinking through the consequences of his actions. You can't charge the dead with criminal intent. There's nothing there," she pointed to her temple, "To indicate thought, ergo there's nothing there to punish. It would be like whipping a rock."

A few minutes past midnight, I heard Rob break through the fence; after hours of pressure, the sheer weight of his still-fresh body had finally been enough to snap the wooden slats. I scrambled to the open window and peeked out from behind the curtain. He lumbered towards the house. Pressed his face against the red bricks, squashing his nose flat.

Peering down from the safety of the first floor, I could smell a fetid, animal tang, underlaid by a touch of the cedar aftershave he'd favoured in life. He didn't smell dead yet. The moon illuminated the garden like a stadium floodlight, picking out small details I'd been too afraid to examine earlier; his blond hair was still relatively neat, streaked with a smattering of dirt. They'd buried him in the electric blue suit he'd worn to prom. I'd worn a dress of a similar colour, although it hadn't been a close enough match to escape his notice.

The breeze changed, flowing back towards him. His head snapped up. Wide eyes, devoid of emotion, fixated on me. His jaws snapped again and again, fruitlessly consuming the night air. I shrank back into my oversized t-shirt, pulling my goose-pimpled limbs into the safety of the cotton cocoon and retreated into the safety of darkness. The sound of clashing teeth died down outside. He returned to smushing his face against the brick wall, emitting a continuous whimper.

Around 3am, my father—wearing only boxers and slippers—leaned out of the living room window and poked Rob with the barrel of a loaded shotgun. I heard a familiar *ka-thunk*, but no shot followed. Rob continued to strain and growl, unwilling or unable to be swayed from his goal. When I slept, it was fitfully; the first bad night I'd had since his funeral, three days before. In the morning, I loaded the blender with healthy fruit and protein powder, while several of the neighbors banded together to haul him out of our yard and chain him to a lamppost at the end of the street. He lunged every few seconds, pulling the chain taut around his neck. His eyes never left our house.

"Can't someone drive him out into the country and dump him there? I don't want to see him every time I leave the house." I picked at the label on my t-shirt, worrying at the loose threads.

"Well, sweetie," my father said, taking off his cap

and wiping sweat from his forehead. "You'll just have to look the other way. He probably doesn't mean any harm. He loved you, that's all. Don't you kids like that sort of thing nowadays?"

"No. And I'm not a kid."

"You know," he continued, as if I hadn't answered, "Your vampire romances and your..." He floundered, trying to think of another creature. "Your Patrick Swayze ghost-types. Your sister's always banging on about how attractive Christian Beige is."

"I don't want Rob anywhere near me, Dad."

My father slung an arm over my shoulders. "Okay. I'll borrow Bill's truck and I'll drive him somewhere tomorrow. Does that make you feel better?"

It didn't, but politeness dictated I should never admit so.

I watched the men load Rob into the back of a truck. He strained against them, glassy eyes fixed on our house. When he was safely ensconced, one of the men slapped the top of the truck and it pulled away from the kerb. Rob began to howl before they'd reached the corner. When the cries had died away, I could still hear the noise echoing in my head. He was gone, I told myself, and that was the end of our relationship. Finally, I was free.

Naturally, Rob returned before dinner the next day, and took up his previous position to the right of our front door.

"It's the damnedest thing," my mother said, smoking out of the open window. "How far did you say you took him, Carl?"

"A good fifty miles." My father heaped a second helping of peas onto his plate. "Fella's like a homing pigeon."

"That doesn't make sense," my sister argued. "He didn't die here. It's not his house."

"He came for me." I leaned against the wall. Three sets of eyes swivelled towards the doorway. "He, uh, texted me. Right before his car crashed. Said he was coming over."

What he'd actually said was something I didn't want to repeat out loud.

"Well, there you go," my father mumbled through a mouthful of potato mash. "Could just be he misses you."

"Didn't you say you broke up with him before he died?" The cigarette between my mother's lips bobbed with every word.

"Yeah, I did."

"Guess it didn't stick." She blew a narrow plume of smoke into the warm night air.

"Guess not."

At first I confined myself to the house, assuming if Rob couldn't see me directly, he might get bored and leave. After a couple of sleepless nights, tossing and turning as the low growl ebbed and flowed through my now-closed window, I moved my stuff to the guest bedroom. The thought of his corpse barnacled to our brickwork, waiting for a chance to invade my home, wasn't a comfortable one. Unfortunately, as soon as I moved, he did too; lurching around the corner of the house, stumbling over dirty boots left at the back door. When he caught sight of me through the kitchen window, his arms windmilled so hard his hand caught in the trellis, and tore two fingers off. My mother went outside, armed with a our grandmother's cast-iron skillet, but Rob only had eyes for me. She sighed as she shovelled the fingers into the garbage.

"At least they don't move of their own accord, right?"

If she was trying to cheer me up, it hadn't worked. I started having nightmares about those fingers crawling through unknown holes in our outer walls, wriggling through gaps or open windows. Writhing under floorboards. I jumped at every shadow, sure I could feel them crawling on me. In life, his fingers had been a source of constant terror for me; they'd squeezed skin, poked soft flesh, texted cruel words, created passive-aggressive social media posts. His fingers had kept me in line. When fingers hadn't been enough, he wasn't above using his whole hand.

My parents had never known about Rob's past behaviour. They treated him now like an irritating but adorable dog who wasn't allowed inside only because it would soil the carpet. My own fear went far deeper. I woke every morning, sour-tongued and sweating, expecting to see his face looming over me. Lacking my usual gym access, I increased the amount I ran on my father's treadmill every morning before breakfast. 3k became 5k. 5k became 10k. Running had once felt like an escape—a sanctioned activity where no one expected me to answer my phone, to be available to handle day-to-day life—and even Rob had approved of this hobby. Now I was trapped, running in place like a terrified rodent.

After two weeks, I cracked. Grabbing my keys, I bolted towards my car and threw myself inside, slamming the door just as Rob's eight remaining fingers smashed against the window. He stooped, gnashing his teeth, staring at my chest. I locked the doors automatically, but he didn't even try the handle. Perhaps he'd forgotten how. Pulling out of the driveway—fighting the urge to simply mow him down and leave him on the concrete slabs for someone else to deal with—I drove into town and bought a smoothie just for something to do. When I arrived home, my parents were watching TV, looking pleased.

"He left when you did. Haven't seen hide nor hair of him since."

Rob turned up less than an hour later.

"He's standing in my begonias, Carl." My mother lit a cigarette without even opening a window.

My father sighed. "Well, what do you want me to do about it?"

I left them to their bickering, aware that on some level this was my fault.

Rob followed me around all summer—to the hairdressers, where he watched a middle-aged woman lather and cut my hair in messy layers while the latest pop music played; to the mall, where I wandered between racks of the latest fashions without seeing anything. Once, I drove over a hundred miles to a Starbucks in the next city over. As I pulled back onto the highway, dirty chai latte safely nestled into the cupholder, I saw a stoop-shouldered figure shambling on the other side of the road. As I overtook him, he pivoted, and began to shuffle in my direction. I watched him in my rear-view mirror so long, I nearly slammed into the Buick in front.

The driver gave me the finger. I didn't retaliate. I deserved as much.

In the first week of autumn, I downloaded a dating app and made lunch plans with a nice systems analyst who bailed the second he saw Rob glowering through the window of the coffee shop. The same thing happened twice more before I learned my lesson and got creative; a date with a doctor on a Ferris wheel, a date with a barista at a zoo. I insisted on picking the date location and never chose a spot with fewer than three exits. Rob hadn't been able to get near me yet, so I didn't know for sure what he'd do if he had the opportunity, but I wasn't taking any chances.

Ironically, the date with a sound engineer in an escape room was the most relaxed I'd felt in a long time. As the clock began the final countdown, I felt my unease creeping back in. The engineer studied the last puzzle on the wall, slender fingers pulling at his short beard, then let out a triumphant yowl. We exited the room while he babbled about how he'd figured out the solution—something to do with Roman numerals—but I couldn't focus. The employee met us in the lobby, smiling brightly, camera held at the ready.

"Well done, guys! Want a photo with your time?" She held up a small whiteboard, the number 54 scrawled in green marker.

"Sure!" The engineer beamed. "Uh, don't you want one?"

Rob was standing outside, staring in through the frosted glass window.

"Okay." I half-turned, "Um, where's your back entrance?"

The employee pointed. "Just down this corridor." She raised the camera. "Ready?"

I smiled as best I could. The engineer's hand snaked around my waist and pulled me closer. Later, I'd check my email and study the photo. Rob's solemn face peeked over my shoulder, as if he'd been photobombing me. The engineer sent a short text thanking me for the pleasant afternoon and inviting me to another date the following week.

I declined.

✳

Eventually, I called the cops. Two turned up, stood with hands on hips, watching Rob crush his face against the wall, red bricks leaving a dimpled impression on his skin. He wasn't sloughing like the others did. Held together by sheer spite, probably.

"Not much we can do for you." The older cop sucked his teeth. "Sorry."

"But he's committing a crime. Surely you can dispose of him? Or return him to the care of his parents? There must be a law abou—"

The cops exchanged looks. "Well, see, he hasn't done anything wrong yet, ma'am. Maybe you should take a little vacation, get yourself calmed down."

"I am calm. I'm telling you, he's stalking me."

"Well, I guess you could choose to see it that way. But it's like, uh..." the younger cop swallowed, "A benign stalking. He ain't tried to hurt you, has he?"

I was so angry I could hardly breathe; the floor rolled under my feet, causing my knees to buckle. I slumped into the nearest chair, feeling like a bathysphere under immense pressure. "I mean—"

"The Supreme Court hasn't made any rulings about dead folks yet," the young cop continued. "They say they want more information before they can start passing laws. This phenomenon is still new to us, and we have to ascertain the true nature of the beast before we can make any real headway." Repeating a speech given by the mayor, word for word. Real smart.

"A woman in Michigan was attacked by her dead ex-husband." I placed my fingers over my eye sockets and pushed, hoping to alleviate the pulsating rage. "I saw it on the news last week. Tore out her throat in front of her kids. The guy was put down. Dismembered. Listen, we've got plenty of shovels. You could do it right now."

"That was a special case," the young cop said, his moustache bristling, "But that's because he attacked her, you know? He actually committed a crime. Or what would have been a crime if he'd been alive, you know? This guy—" he pointed his radio antennae towards Rob, "He's just kinda... following you around."

"That's what stalking is."

"When it's a live person, sure, that's stalking."

"But when it's a dead person, it's not?" I decided

to change tack. "Fine. Can't I get a restraining order or something?"

The older cop leaned towards me and patted my shoulder in a paternal way. "Look, ma'am. We understand you're distressed by this, but he hasn't done anything wrong as such."

"Yet." Silence. I gave up and let my hands fall into my lap. "So, what? You're gonna wait until he's murdered me before you do anything? How is that supposed to help me?"

The cops exchanged glances again and rose as one. "Call us if the situation changes."

Lawyers wouldn't take my case. The press wouldn't listen. Even my own family were starting to get tired of my complaints. Every day on the news I saw more and more violence enacted by dry-earthers—CNN's 'fun nickname' for the newcomers—against regular people. A salesman in Mexico City, bitten to death by his ex-wife in a food court in front of his three children. An estate agent in Munich, devoured by her dead fiancée. A vet in Johannesburg, murdered on the job while the litter of puppies he'd been vaccinating wagged their tails and barked joyfully. Theories sprang up: dry-earthers went after the people they'd most loved in life. Dry-earthers went after the people they'd secretly hated. Dry-earthers attacked familiar smells. The truth was, nobody really knew. And I had no intention of finding out.

I applied for, and got, a decent job in Washington. Gave my sister all the clothes I couldn't fit in my suitcase. Kissed my parents goodbye like I was a normal person moving across the country for a normal reason. They made me promise to call every week. I wondered how long until they saw me on the news.

Rob walked almost eleven hundred miles in two weeks and turned up just as I was about to sign the paperwork to adopt a kitten; his shoes had worn through and the bones of his feet clacked against the pavement. I fled without completing the adoption process, retreated into my new, 'dry-safe' apartment. Burrowed back into my old ways. The doormen were trained not to let him into the building, and to walk me outside whenever I chose to leave, which wasn't often these days. I had all my food delivered. I did my job remotely, working long hours. I bought my own treadmill.

Months passed. Sensing I had lost focus, but keen to retain my skillset, the company offered me the option to relocate to Canada. I jumped at the chance.

Rob walked there too. The snow during the winter months slowed him down, but he still turned up everywhere I went. I paid a vet a hundred dollars in cash to microchip him, and had the tracking map pulled up at all times on every device I owned.

Wherever I went, Rob followed. Eventually, I applied for a visa and moved to London. The small green blip on my tracking map crawled across the page, one millimetre at a time. My parents begged me to come home for Thanksgiving; I made plausible excuses. As a compromise, I flew home mid-March for two weeks. In my childhood bedroom I woke up drenched in sweat and shaking, expecting to see him outside, to smell the particular scent of cedar and rot. I'd lost weight. My skin was paler, always slightly clammy to the touch. The blip on my screen moved towards me no matter where I was in the world.

In London, I started therapy. I met a guy, fell in love, got engaged. He understood my predicament to begin with, but as the years wore on, I checked the map more and more frequently. Here was Rob, a blip halfway across the Atlantic Ocean. Here was Rob, emerging from the sea onto the rocky beach at Blackpool. Here was Rob, breaching the outskirts of London. Adamantly making a bee-line for me, regardless of where I was. As inexorable as death itself. Time to fly home to the US for a month and let the whole hideous process begin again.

My fiancé watched me over the top of his canvas;

charcoal in one hand, glass of whisky in the other. "Suze, don't you think this thing has gone on long enough? You check the map every hour. You don't sleep through the night any more. Don't you think it's time to move on?"

"There's no such thing."

"As closure?" He scoffed. "Come on. Don't be ridiculous. He's never even touched you. How bad could it be?"

I didn't know how to explain to him that Rob was going to be the death of me, and I knew that even if I expressed this notion out loud, he wouldn't believe me until it had actually happened. By which point, it would be too late.

A couple of months later, he started sleeping on the couch. Three months after that, he left for an evening with some friends and never came home again. I saw his social media posts, happy and smiling, photographs taken in enclosed spaces with a girl who looked like I'd used to.

"You've got a heart murmur. You need to lower your blood pressure," my doctor said. "Meditate. More vegetables. Do you smoke?"

"No."

"Hmm. Exercise?"

"Six times a week." I sat back in my chair. "How bad is the murmur?"

The doctor made a seesawing motion with her left hand. "Could be worse. Could be better. The stress isn't helping." She skimmed my file again.

"What are my options?"

"Valve repair or replacement. Pretty standard, comes with all the usual risks but you're young and healthy. We feel sure you'll have a routine procedure and a full recovery. The science is very advanced these days. Practically routine." She reached into the bowl on her desk, selected a lemon sherbet, and unwrapped the candy. "Sugar-free sweet?"

"No, thank you. Would it be possible to have a full heart transplant?"

She stared at me, crunching the remnants. The scent of lemon, heady and hot, wafted across the desk. "I think you misunderstand me, Ms Thomas. You don't need one."

"Hear me out."

A young man with an aversion to seatbelts provided my new heart. I felt relief as they wheeled me into the operating room; either way, I'd be free of Rob forever.

Getting a new heart was tough. Getting them to agree to hand over my old one was even harder. They kicked up a fuss, but I won in the end. Extenuating circumstances and all that. Seeing Rob loitering at the front of the hospital convinced even the most conservative medical professionals.

My sister flew in to assist me while I recovered. Two years later, she no longer found his attentions romantic; yelling at him when she took out the recycling, hitting him with the handle of a broom the help usually reserved for sweeping the communal hallways. Once I'd gained my full strength back, I dipped into my savings and scoured the internet. A couple of enquiries later, I found what I was looking for.

"But your heart, Suzanne," my sister said, pulling damp clothes from the washing machine and passing them over. "It's your heart. Just because—I mean, like, no man has a right to it. No entitlement whatsoever. It's your heart, after all. There has to be another way."

"Don't be fooled." I hung up a sock. "The heart isn't the seat of the soul. The brain is the real throne. A heart is just an organ. The real me is in every fibre, every cell. I could basically replace every atom in my body one by one, and I'd still be the original me. Only now, I'd have a useful decoy. It's basically the Ship of Theseus argument."

She waved an airy hand. "You know I don't watch any of those pirate shows." Shoving a whole biscuit in her mouth, she chewed thoughtfully while I repressed a smile. "Does Rob know all this?"

"I damn well hope not."

"What do you think?" the pilot yelled. "You wanna go further?"

"This is perfect, thank you." I yanked the lid off the container and took the heart out. The organ lay in my palm, surprisingly heavy, and much paler than I'd expected it to be. I secured myself to the wall with a hook, and lobbed the damn thing out of the window. It spiralled downwards and disappeared among the waves with barely a splash.

The pilot craned over his shoulder. "Nice shot."

"Shouldn't you be watching where we're going?"

He gestured at the empty horizon. "Not a lot of traffic up here." He chewed on his lip for a moment. "You okay?"

I considered. "I think I might be happy."

"Oh yeah?" His round face crumpled in disbelief. "Didn't you just literally throw your heart into the ocean? Doesn't sound like the happiest thing to me."

"It wasn't working." I could no longer tell where the heart had disappeared, and my chest had begun to feel warm and tingly. "Sometimes you need to change the situation. Sometimes you need to change yourself."

He shrugged, unconvinced.

＃

The blip stayed in the Atlantic Ocean for days, then weeks, then months. I checked less and less as time wore on. A year later, I couldn't remember when I'd last looked at it; panicking, I pulled the map up, my fingers slick on the laptop keyboard. The blip was in the same place. He'd be there forever now. Rob had got what he thought he wanted, and I'd finally won my freedom.

THIEF

(published by Orchid's Lantern)

Crooked trees beckon you like fingers. Bark wrinkles like elderly hands in motion. You walk on the path, lemon sherberts crunching under your boots. Yellow shards, coating your soles. Cherry drops coo from high above; their young are barely more than red dots, hiding behind their parent's wrappers. Foil coins hang from branches as long as school rulers. You fill your pockets with strawberry bonbons until your blazer weighs as much as a lie. Cram mint humbugs into your mouth, between gum and cheek. Class hamster-cute.

On the beach, a pink piggy bank—twice the size of a truck—naps, half-buried, in the sand. It is labelled.

This is not your name. You drop to your knees and scrape away the wet sludge. The coin slot is exposed. You fit your arm inside. You grope around. It is empty.

Twenty yards out from the shore, another pink piggy bank is drowning. You wade into the creamy waves. The cola water fizzes around your calves. You dive down. You pick starfish off the sides, peeling them back limb by limb. This piggy bank is labelled too. This is not your name. Nothing rattles inside. No sunken treasure. No chest of dark jewels or gold coins stamped with different kings or strings of milky pearls or silver goblets or gem-encrusted daggers. Nothing you can sell or trade. Breaking the surface of the waves, you stumble to your feet. Your face dripping with carbonated shame.

You glance back at the shoreline, wondering if it's not too late. It is too late. The trees have lurched onto the beach to watch. Faces made of nested leaves. Each expression shucked from the last like dead skin. Scabbed wounds, which have never really healed. Too dense to understand your drive. Too compact to understand your need.

You were greedy, once. You were greedy. Weren't you?

A BEGINNER'S GUIDE TO THE
HEAVY PETTING ZOO

The zoo didn't park the car and come to the door, like I thought it might. Instead, a long blast on the horn demanded my presence outside. When I slid into the car, the zoo leaned over— a lithe, tabby serpent emerging from its front door— and moistened my face with a long, dramatic kiss in lieu of a greeting.

"Hey," the zoo added afterwards, windows shuttering briefly at chest height.

"Hey yourself."

The zoo spent most of the drive bitching about work while the radio was turned up too high for me to comfortably catch every word. We arrived in the underground car park of the cinema complex before I'd had a chance to contribute to the conversation. Pulling into a dimly-lit parking space next to a thick white pillar, the zoo yanked on the handbrake then leaned in again and entangled me in another kiss; this time a rhinoceros, the colour of scuffed silver, pressed a horned beak into the side of my neck. I put a hand on the zoo's right wing, where the sound of chirping macaques intermingled with howler monkeys, and pushed it gently away.

"You want to get some popcorn?" I asked, unbuckling my seat belt and checking my lipstick in the wing mirror.

The zoo sighed. The scent of muddy straw and greasy fur wafted towards me. "Yeah, sure."

I got a large sweet popcorn and a small soda, no ice, while the zoo dithered between nachos and nothing. Eventually, I offered to share my popcorn just to hurry the process up. The screen was already dark by the time we found our seats. The zoo took the first handful of popcorn and dropped it down into its red-carpeted entrance. Distantly, a big cat roared. Someone in the row behind shushed us.

"Relax," the zoo muttered. "It's only the trailers."

The zoo paused its chatter when the opening credits appeared, the projection of the age certificate trembling at the edges. I hadn't really wanted to see this particular film, having missed the first two in the franchise, but the zoo had called my other choices boring. Besides, this was a summer blockbuster. I was assured of a pleasant, if rather formulaic, experience. During a protracted car chase, I nipped to the bathroom, only to find on my return that the zoo had finished my popcorn.

Afterwards, we strolled out. The zoo held the door open for me. A market stall in a tight suede jacket flashed me a sidelong glance—little more than a subliminal blink—before her boyfriend came out of the toilets, all quaffed hair and Yeezys, and started sucking on her merchandise display.

The question came before we reached the car. "Do you want to come back to mine?"

I declined. I had work in the morning, and a big meeting mid-afternoon, which I exaggerated out of all proportion. In truth, the film's constant use of shakycam had left me feeling nauseous and off-kilter. "Maybe next time?"

"Sure." The loud radio didn't cover the awkward silence. The zoo dropped me on the main road, making some excuse about three-point turns at this time of night, and zoomed off before I could even wave goodbye.

I decided I wouldn't see the zoo again, no matter how interesting the animals were, but after another week of alternating between different screens—from Excel to an online vendor management system to Netflix to Prime and back again—I was overcooked on extroversion and starved for physical touch. When the zoo texted *hey r u doing anything thursday?* I set a timer for twenty minutes and finished off my cardio workout before responding. Delayed gratification served several purposes, but mainly made me feel as if I was in control of my limited choices.

On Wednesday night, Hannah and Thom came over for our usual mid-week dinner. She spotted a sexy black blouse I'd laid out over a chair for my upcoming booty call. "Are you still seeing the zoo? I thought you'd phased that out."

I pulled a face. "Yeah, tomorrow. I was going to, but like—I don't know. It's just—"

"Easy?" Thom suggested.

"No. God, no." I thought of the way I loved having my hair pulled in bed but somehow the zoo always managed to yank it at the wrong angle. I thought of the too-loud radio, the feeling as if I might as well be a woman-shaped lump of jelly in the passenger seat for all the zoo noticed or cared. "Definitely not easy."

"Never is." Hannah poured herself a little more wine.

"Can't be that bad if you keep shagging it." Thom reached for another piece of garlic bread, chewing with his mouth slightly ajar. A piece of crust rotated behind his teeth, tumbling like a lonely sock in a washing machine.

Hannah and I exchanged looks. He forced a

"what?" out through a mouthful of crushed carbs.

She put down her fork. "Up for an experiment?"

Thom chewed again, swallowed. Smirked. "Depends."

She got up and moved around the table, leaning over his shoulder. His eyes followed her outstretched hand as she placed another piece of garlic bread on his plate. "Okay, so you're hungry, right?"

"Yeah." he said, warily. "Obviously."

Hannah lifted the first piece of bread to his mouth. "Bite."

He obeyed. She twirled a few ribbons of spaghetti on his fork, and offered them. He clamped his mouth around the fork and sucked, cheeks hollowing. She picked up the bread again. "Another bite."

"But I haven't fin—" he began to protest.

She pushed it against his lips.

He bit, beginning to look uncomfortable. "More," she said. "Take more than that." He did so. "More. Come on, you want to make me happy, yeah? Have another." She pushed the bread harder against his lips. He turned his head but she grabbed his cheek, clamped her fingers against his stubble, bent down until they were eye to eye.

"If you're hungry, a meal's a meal, right?" His jaw was still working rapidly, his throat bobbing as she spoke. "There's no difference between eating this at your own pace and having someone keep forcing another bite into your mouth when you're not done chewing or swallowing the first, right?" She crushed the garlic bread against his lips. Butter oozed down his chin. "You're enjoying it all the same, right?"

Thom choked, spluttered, pushed back his chair. Bent over, coughing. Hannah dropped the garlic bread onto the plate and retreated back to her chair, wiping her hands on a napkin.

"Yeah, but—" he wheezed, cheekbones purpling with the effort. "You could just say no. Like, say no thanks, I'm full."

Hannah lifted her wine and raised an eyebrow at me.

I speared a lump of beef. "What makes you think we don't?"

I turned up at the zoo's apartment after work on Thursday with a bottle of red wine. The zoo met me at the door in nothing but a loose robe, the animals already cacophonous, and I barely managed to make it to the kitchen while it pawed at my sweater.

"Let's get you out of these clothes, hmm?"

I found two clean hi-ball glasses in a cupboard, standing out like tall poppies in a   field of novelty mugs. "Don't you want something to drink?"

"I can think of better things to taste," it purred, shepherding me into the bedroom.

I knew from experience this wasn't true—the zoo often sexted me about how much it wanted to go down on me, but had yet to actually do so when given the chance.

My male friends often joked publicly about how little time they took in bed—my female friends privately wished they'd hurry it up. "There's no use hammering away for twenty minutes if the electric drill only has one speed, know what I'm saying?" Lou had said, while Hannah nodded. "What good does it do to cut a few planks if you're not going to sand them down afterwards, or add some varnish?"

I'd been quite drunk at the time, so the metaphors had largely escaped me, but lying pinned under the zoo once more, I was forcibly reminded that horniness could drive a person to endure really uncomfortable things. A beaver with scarlet gums, protruding from the zoo's gift shop, nibbled at a sensitive spot at the base of my neck. Its broad head was spotted with pale blotches, the colour of uncooked halloumi. I was suddenly ravenous.

"Hold on. Can I just," I adjusted my position as much as I could without actually moving. "Um. Your parking lot is on my hair."

"Oh, okay." The zoo shifted its weight, brushing my hair off the pillow and into my eyes. "You good?"

"I mean, actually—"

The beaver's square pupils shrank. The zoo sighed.

"Yeah, no, I'm good." I lay back, feeling the sharp edges of the ticket booth digging into my ribs, and did my best to focus on my own pleasure. As the minutes ticked back, I grew more and more numb. The bones of my fingers clicked, and I wondered whether this was the start of early-onset arthritis. The zoo shuddered unexpectedly, groaned, and rolled off. "That was great. You good?"

I gazed down the length of my own body; ZOO was imprinted in red letters across my abdomen. "Not yet."

The zoo leaned closer, rubbed its sweaty roof on the shell of my ear, whispered all its fantasies into my ear. Not my fantasies, not even close—just the things the zoo sexted me at 3am or sometimes 3pm, tired of the grind of daily life. I ignored the stream of filth and focused on the noises; a powerful trumpet, a pack of stampeding hooves, chirps and bellows and bleats and —

I half-finished, feeling like a marathon runner who'd crumpled to the ground ten feet from the finish line and was being dragged over it by others. The climax left me with distant, coastal-green grief roiling in my stomach; big, billowing waves, like a painted storm. I gave the zoo a last sloppy kiss and started hunting for my socks.

"Are you into this?" the zoo asked. Its tone was curious, rather than hurt or disappointed.

I felt a prickle, curving up my spine. It was hard to explain—even though I'd done so multiple times over the last few years to a chandler's, a cheesemongers, a German Christmas market stall, and a small, niche modern art gallery. I wanted to say *yes, I did want to fool around, but I meant when it happens naturally, with chemistry.* I wanted to say *could you possibly try treating me like a human instead of a choose-your-own-adventure game with your finger on the final page.* I wanted to say *how hard is it, really, to notice that someone else actually exists and isn't just an orbital moon to your Very Important Planet?*

I bit my lip. "The thing is, I'm really busy at the moment and I don't really have a lot of time for me, you know? So, like, maybe best that we just end things. On a good note."

A colony of ants—New York pink, with french speckles—marched over the zoo's roof, following an invisible path. I braced myself for an outburst, but the zoo merely stared at me. "Okay." It shrugged.

"Okay?"

"Yeah, mate. You do you."

I gathered my things together and laced up my boots. The zoo walked me to the door and leaned against the chipped green paint, fingered a flake. "See you."

"Uh, yeah. Bye." I zipped my rain jacket up to the chin, the chill of the stone walls already permeating the thin denim of my jeans.

"Hey, Aly?" The zoo called. Cage doors clanged. Something bubbled—the sound of a river creature, drowning.

I turned.

The zoo smiled. "Thanks for coming."

MINERAL BOUQUET

(published by Twist in Time magazine)

All hail the true one, as the true one hails us. May the society be pleased to receive the enclosed selection of notes from one Dr Smiley, 'ae Greate Lovere Of Winnes', as presented from her diaries. As we all know, diary-keeping was, in the early years of the Ascendance. a very popular hobby, given the largely indoor nature of the lives led in this time period. We cannot ascertain much about Dr Smiley's other proclivities, but we know in excellent detail the state of her tongue and liver. All hail the true one, as the true one hails us. We are missing many sections from these notes - in particular, the loss of the Cretaceous period is a real shame - but we hope to obtain a fuller flavour of the text, should the society vote to *permit us to use The Machine. We have selected a lab assistant to sacrifice, should the society grant us this wish. The lab assistants have not been informed which of them has been selected, as pending doom tends to make them ferrety and nervous. Please do not leave the platform. Let us begin. All hail the true one, as the true one hails us.*

JURASSIC

A medium red

A full-throated satisfaction. Dew-soaked piles of rubies, afforded the respect they deserve. A drum in the distance indicates that you are too late. The hunt began hours ago. You saved your own skin but at the cost of your conscience. You may now cut out and consume this (located just under your right collarbone) as it will become toxic in a matter of hours. Burying it at a crossroads will not stop your conscience from hunting you down. Your conscience never sleeps, never breathes. It cannot smell silver or taste garlic.

Pair with: deer haunch, with the teeth marks of your favourite hunting dog still imprinted on the flesh. Cat-lovers may struggle with anything larger than pudús. Rub down with an Icelandic black lava salt-cube for an invigorating pyroclastic tingle.

TRIASSIC

A deep red

Silky, buttoned-down, and intellectually satisfying, especially for those who feel the Jurassic period is beneath them or too flashily modern; one must ignore the cries of one's colleagues and ex-lovers who have theorised that the brevity of the taste somehow reflects poorly on one's own life choices, and who would do WELL to look at their own vintners before throwing glass bottles, ROBERT.   T h i s e r a i s particularly beguiling to lovers of mammalian lifeforms. Hot and bloody on the palate. Plenty of rushed tannins. Chewy but short-lived. Much like a certain physical activity I could mention which we used to enjoy together, ROBERT, but which you now partake of solely with unascended, miserable, interchangable widows, so miserable and interchangeable that I refuse to even learn their names in order to hate them properly.

Pair with: duck breast, coiffed and preened, inside a whole citrus peel. Stand alone on a well-lit stage with a half-lit audience. Wait until the murmurs have grown uneasy. Use a syringe to pipe it in. Don't break the skin. Don't shatter the illusion.

All hail the true one, as the true one hails us. May the society accept our apologies that we could not ascertain who Robert was, despite sacrificing two lab assistants to the beast which currently inhabits the book vault. Dr Smiley, by her own admission, is ae Great Lovere Of Winnes but perhaps not ae Great Admirer of Menne, or at least one particular manne. All hail the true one, as the true one hails us.

PERMIAN

A blanc-de-blanc

Glacial rivers. Tectonic plates which used to grind together but which have now parted, leaving a cold chasm where once a stomach wound elegantly around a heart.

All hail the true one, as the true one hails us. We are missing the pairing of the Permian section, but the reference to the placement of the stomach leads us to believe that Dr Smiley was reasonably well-versed as to the placement of human organs after the Ascendance. There would, after all, have been thousands of bodies lying around in the streets like overripe fruit from laden trees. Scientific experimentation was plentiful during this period. We shall not bore the society with what it already knows. All hail the true one, as the true one hails us. Regarding the question of whether or not humans were generally aware that, prior to the Ascendance, our stomachs were usually found below our hearts, is a long-standing debate in our community. Efforts to reverse the natural order of unascended subjects has not been greatly successful. *We apologise for our continued interruptions. All hail the true one, as the true one hails us.*

CARBONIFEROUS

Pinot Noir

The immediate floral bouquet of the Pennsylvanian elevates what might have been a simple Mississippian marine transgression; a trace amount of ancient salt left in the shell after the tide has been swallowed. You recall a time a childhood friend died of dehydration, having miscalculated the amount of water required for a hike. Hot days find you pouring Evian out by the side of the road. You slosh out as much as you took from her that day to impress a boy. A libation to love.

Pair with roasted pine nuts, blow-dried on a bed of damp kale. Lowest setting advised. Serve whatever kale has remained on the plate; this is the good-old-boy kale, the bootstrap kale, the kale to which other kale must aspire to be considered worthy of kale rights. Kale rights are not free. To think otherwise is perverse, the sure sign of a populated mind. Encourage your dining companions to check each other's facial orifices, particularly the ears, for kale-creatures. If anyone has been Taken, let groupthink do all the heavy lifting here.

DEVONIAN

A white demi-sec

The finish is acorn-rounded, cloven-hoofed. A foxy stroll through a forest in autumn, maple leaves turning various shades of wounds. The sudden realisation that you have married into a clan who is at this moment polishing their hunting weaponry and planning your demise. They must play by the rules but you, an outsider, do not have to.

Embrace this opportunity; use the chaos to your advantage to avenge yourself for that dig in Cousin Barbara's speech at Tim's wedding last year. She thought she could pass it off as a light-hearted pun, but you know her sly ways. She undermined you and now she has to taste the sweet dish at any goddamn temperature you want to serve it. They will respect you for it afterwards. One day, you will rise to the exalted position of matriarch. One day, they will cower in your shadow. One day, you will rule this entire family. One day, you will replace all these ancient, flickering hall lamps, because they cannot possibly be environmentally friendly. For now, there's only you, Barb, and the knife on the floor between you. Do not hesitate. Seize your moment. Seize your destiny. Recycle that bitch.

Pair with: chicken fillet drizzled in a rosemary and thyme sauce. Arrange carrots (julienne, not sliced, you are not a monster) in the name of your dinner guest along the edge of the plate. You may gain additional respect - but lose personal touches - if you simply write BARB on each one. It works as a threat on multiple levels.

SILURIAN

A sweet white

A foggy ship deck. Eerie noises bubble just under the surface of the water; they detonate in a series of small bursts, like belches pleading for rescue. This is a maiden voyage propelled entirely by blushes and the naive expectations of having heard what it is to lie with a man. It is, in reality, quite different; the duet shorter, the after-aria lonelier than before. You awake in the dusk. You stumble to the basin and immerse your whole head. You emit several wracked, coppery coughs into your grandfather's handkerchief; the firelight illuminates the thickened, cassandric contents of your lungs, which up until now you believed to have been free of the Disease.

Pair with: something which you have caught on a line woven from your mother's hair and your own; ignore the creature's feeble protests. Ae Dirre Warninge: do not let it sing. To hear the song is death, to hear the song will eclipse your own Ascendance. Let those take note who wish to learn from my own errors.

All hail the true one, as the true one hails us. We believe that we could, with use of The Machine, restore the text to its original form. Samantha will give her life for this. We have decided. Please do not leave the platform, Samantha. Cease your struggling. The kind donation of your life will advance the knowledge of humanity, or at least, what is left of it. We invite the society to vote regarding our request. I repeat... I repeat... Samantha, they cannot hear me over your screams. This is very impolite. The society does not tolerate impoliteness. We invite the society to vote regarding our request. All hail the true one, as the true one hails us.

GLEAN

(published by Bag of Bones)

Winter, Year One
Mum says we need to start thinking about the future. The herd needs to multiply, whether they want to or not.

Winter, Year Two
Cows don't plough well but they're all we have. The old man next door traded us a whole heap of winter clothes for just one cow. Mum laughed and said the guy was thinking with his pin bone, but I didn't get the joke. I still don't.

Winter, Year Three

Mum let me pick the straws to choose which cow she slaughters. I thought it would feel easier that way, but it didn't. A couple died of the flu last month; we had to burn their bodies in case it spread.

Winter, Year Four

They trust me because I sneak them extra feed. Now that I'm almost grown, Mum lets me groom them. I sing to them sometimes. They get scared easily but I think they like my songs—especially Daisy.

Winter, Year Five

Mum says I have to kill my first one this year. Says she needs to know I've got the stomach for it, to continue on if anything happens to her.

Winter, Year Six

A cow ran away with her calf. Mum strung them up in the yard as a warning to the rest. The herd won't let me anywhere near them now, not even Daisy. Last time I tried, she bit me.

Winter, Year Seven

I lied. We never owned cows.

ELMO'S STRUGGLE

(published by Catapult)

Sesame Street was pleasant on this sunny morning, as it was every morning. The keen light illuminating the brownstones opposite my window thrilled me as it ever did. I breakfasted before heading outside, and the chatter of high voices pulled me in a northerly direction. Zoe and Gabi were standing by the nearest lamppost, talking about their favourite clouds. Gabi was wearing a red t-shirt, tucked neatly into her jeans. Close to the colour of my fur, but not an exact match.

"Hi," I said.

They chorused, "Hi, Elmo!"

Gabi smiled at me. I smiled back.

"We were just talking about what to do today," Gabi said. "Let's go to the beach."

Zoe's hand snaked out, holding a grey rock at eye level. "Rocco wants to go swimming." She tilted her head, as if listening. "He says he's the world's greatest swimmer. Way better than any of us."

"Rocco can't swim," I said.

All eyes turned to me.

"You've never seen him swim," Zoe pointed out. "How do you know what he can do?"

"Because he's a rock."

"So?" She moved her hand a little closer to my face, forcing me to contemplate the pitted rock. "Are you scared that Rocco will beat you?"

It wasn't worth arguing so early in the day. "Okay," I said. "Elmo will go to the beach too."

No one had yet asked me what my favourite kind of cloud was, and as we packed a large wicker basket full of picnic treats, it occurred to me that likely the conversation had been forgotten. Bitterness rankled. Probably somebody had asked Rocco what his favourite kinds of clouds were.

By the time we arrived at the beach, the sun was high in the sky. Cumulus clouds scudded past, obscuring the light for only a brief moment before bounding off to seek larger adventures. Above them, ponderous stratocumulus hovered like anxious babysitters. Our shadows were little more than slender, dark puddles at our feet; definition, without shape. The beach was otherwise deserted. Gulls screeched in the distance, circling something I couldn't see.

I sighed, my heart swelling with appreciation for the view. The harsh beauty of the sea, contrasted against the stoic, pale sand, never failed to rouse a deep and profound feeling of calm. Gabi laid the red plaid picnic blanket down on the grass and set the basket down beside it. I picked the spot nearest her and made to sit down, but Zoe flung herself onto the blanket first, declaring that Rocco wanted to lie in the exact middle so he would feel safe. She placed the rock down reverentially and it sank into a slight depression, whiskering the blanket on all sides.

I raised my eyes heavenwards for a moment, seeking strength in the blue expanse. Let her have her foolish notions. I would not let her trouble me today. And yet—

"Rocco says he's the greatest swimmer ever, right?" I said, wriggled into my water-wings. "Elmo and Rocco can race to the water and see if Rocco is right."

"Oh, Rocco can't race you on land," Zoe said, absorbed in applying sunscreen to Rocco. Her fingers stroked the rock, ensuring every crack and crevice was slathered. She smiled and patted it, as one might do with a particularly well-behaved dog. "He needs a little help getting to the sea."

I chewed on my lip fur. "If he can't even walk to

the water, how can he possibly—"

"Some people need help on land, Elmo," Gabi said. "Water allows us to float. Gravity is lessened in water. When people have car accidents or need to learn how to reuse a broken leg, gentle exercises in water can strengthen their muscles without putting any strain —"

But Rocco doesn't have legs." My fists were clenched. I took a deep breath.

"It's not polite to point out what people are missing, Elmo." Gabi smiled without malice. "We talked about this."

I splayed my feet out, watching the sand rise between my furry toes. Soft, yet gritty. "Okay, Gabi."

Zoe took off, racing towards the sea. I sprinted after her, hampered by the awkward bulge of my water-wings around my pistoning arms.

"Go, Rocco!" She spun the rock in her hand and launched it out to sea.

I plunged into the water. A wave slapped my face with cold fingers. I swam a few feet towards the horizon, before turning back. Zoe was standing by the shore, foaming tide lapping around her ankles. In her hand was Rocco.

I licked salt from my lips and bobbed in the water, letting the waves guide my body. I was seeing red; I swept my wet fur out of my eyes. "How did you do that?"

"How's the water?" Zoe called, ignoring my

question, and then without waiting for an answer, swung Rocco into the air once more. The rock struck the water, a mere foot from my head.

Again I dived under, pushing against the natural buoyancy of the water-wings, hoping to catch the arc of the rock, but on the ocean floor there was only seaweed, streaming in the current like trees under heavy winds.

When I surfaced, gasping for air, Rocco was back in Zoe's hand and her fur was wet. The water did nothing to cool my agita—what did she gain from tormenting me in this fashion? I, who had only ever been a dear friend to her. I, who had indulged so many of my friends and neighbours in their conceits over the years. Resentment tugged at my chest, as weighty as the ocean itself, and I knew that if I stayed for a moment longer, the provocation would cause me to lose my temper.

I thrashed my way back to the shore, water-wings hindering my progress rather than helping it, and made some half-hearted excuse about being hungry already. I trudged back towards the picnic blanket, leaving a trail of splattered wet sand in my wake.

Gabi was lying down on the blanket, sunglasses perched on top of her head. Her eyes were closed and her mouth was slack. I wasn't sure whether she was asleep or not.

"Gabi?"

The answer came without a pause. "Yes, Elmo?"

"Elmo is just curious . . ." I sat down on the blanket, cross-legged, and began to peel off my water-wings. "You know how a speck of dirt can get inside a clam?"

"Uh huh."

I set the water-wings aside, but left them partially inflated, in case I later wanted another dip. I took a sandwich from the wicker basket and bit off a corner. "And you know how a clam can turn a speck of dirt into a shiny pearl?"

Gabi nodded, eyes still closed. "Isn't that a wonderful thing? Nature is full of miracles."

"Mmhmm." I chewed. The bread was fresh, the sweetness of the cheese offset by the tart acidity of the onion chutney.

"Nobody would be interested in the dirt on its own," she continued. "But the evolution of the dirt into something full of lustre makes it interesting and valuable."

"Sure," I said.

In the distance, Zoe's figure bent and straightened, bent and straightened, before she lifted both hands high above her head. The fingers were splayed upwards, towards the sun. She whooped, then shrieked a few words, although I could not make out what was said. Several feet away from where she stood, a tiny grey speck lay discarded on the pale sand. Was it forgotten, or a willing witness to her games? Impossible to tell.

"But isn't a lie kind of a dirty thing too?"

"What do you mean?" Gabi didn't change position, but her jaw tightened.

"This thing with Rocco—"

"Oh, Elmo!" She gestured, hands flapping in exasperation. "We've been over this. Rocco is—"

"Not alive," I cut in.

"Rocco is what Rocco is." She lay back. "Rocco has just as much right to anything as you or I, in Zoe's eyes."

"Elmo thinks a lie is like a speck of dirt," I pressed. "It isn't worth anything. It's only when people pay attention to it, and build upon it, that the lie becomes something different. Sometimes when something is beautiful, Elmo thinks we can forget that it can also be dangerous. And sometimes when something is super fun to pretend, we might forget that it isn't actually real. Isn't that right, Gabi?"

She was silent, although her eyes softened. She took my free hand, which I clutched with fervour.

"Elmo knows Zoe loves Rocco," I said, desperation creeping into my voice. "But please, tell Elmo that you don't reall—"

A silhouette slid onto my feet. Zoe stood, dripping, Rocco in her hand. "What's that about Rocco?"

"Elmo and Gabi were just talking about how Rocco is like a pearl," I said, staring at the wet rock in her hand. A smudge of dark seaweed dangled from the bottom of the stone. Ridged, like a dragon's tail. "Do you hear that? You're a pearl, Rocco."

Zoe smiled; orange delight, mixed with yellow malice. A deep honey hue, neither one thing nor another; a sticky cruelty—peculiarly her own—made just for me.

"Aww, thanks Elmo!"

"No problem," I said, and helped myself to another sandwich. The cheese which I had so much enjoyed only moments before sucked all the remaining moisture from my tongue; I mouthed my own name, in a vain attempt to unstick myself.

My shadow had lengthened, elongated into a tall, grotesque figure. A mockery of my small stature, and no true reflection of my person, as something was dragging it by the fur back towards the sea. I thought again of the seaweed, and how easy it would be to drown in that underwater forest, with no one around but a rock to hear my cries. The sky above was choked with cumulus, and not a single cirrus cloud could be seen.

THE FIRST STARFISH WAS BORN DURING THE ORDOVICIAN PERIOD

Except they're not starfish, they're sea stars, because they don't have gills or fins or tails, just five identical legs, so there is no north or south direction to a starfish—I mean, a sea star—cause it's all just one large endless cycle of ups and down, peaks and troughs, and when you think about it, that's either amazing or nauseating, and a starfish—not a sea star—is slang for a sexual partner who just lies there splayed out and makes no effort, and you've got to wonder why they don't name the person crawling all over the unmoving creature, and I recently found out that that the collective noun for a group of starfish is a galaxy, which sounds beautiful until you really think about it, because a galaxy is full of huge empty spaces between tiny particles of matter, like good days in between months of silent treatment, and it makes me wonder why, if the starfish—I mean, the sea star—has eyes on the end of every arm, why can't I see anything to love in your face any more?

THE WIFE-HUNTERS

(published by Twin Pies)

The wife-hunters are hidden in the long grass. Their scent carries without need of a breeze —a pulsing cloud of back-slapping belt-swagger thick enough to swallow. The season has been a lean one so far, with only a couple of my herd picked off. I've seen these captured sisters moving through the street between the boarded-up houses, clad in yellow cloth, their antlers hidden by soft knit caps. They foal their young behind closed doors. Fire now takes what we would have drowned, given the chance, in our own throats.

The young men are ravenous. Starvation spikes their dark, damp hair, shapes their teeth into savage spirals. Today might be the day they'll bag their own spouses. Hearing the stories, their future sons will puff their scarlet chests out, inflamed with pride. Their future daughters will escape from lazily-tied leashes, long legs lapping up the ground between town and flock. While there will be a few years of growth and maturation between escape and capture, girls understand upon arrival that we have never really been unchained. One noose, simply exchanged for another, looser one. Eventually, it must tighten again.

I press my muzzle to the ground, antlers snagged in dark branches. The herd shift around me, unwilling to desert one of their one. I hiss, pray with libations of cold sweat to go unnoticed, but the men have periscope eyes for every hint and subtle clue. I hiss again and the herd slide away, fading into the darkness beyond the trees, leaving only the smell of fresh-chewed grass. The men approach, no longer bothering to hide, holding guns taut between their thighs. Every barrel is aimed at me; my spotted hide, my long jaws, the elegance arch of a neck not yet bent or broken.

I am spineless, terror-limp, and they handle me like the dead weight of pre-cut meat. They check my hooves, one leg at a time, crowding and probing. They open my mouth, spin a finger inside, look past my gift teeth into the cavern of my chest and send a canary down into the shaft, small, bloodied claws descending by degrees. The bird flutters, betrays me by sending up one plume of purple smoke. The men smile, and sound me out for resonance, tapping a soft-headed hammer on the notches of my spine.

"She's ripe," they murmur. "She's ripe."

Impossible, I know. I rotted, seconds before I was caught.

I AM A MONGOLIAN DEATH WORM
(published by Bear Creek Gazette)

n the arid dunes of the Gobi desert, I burrow under the surface to wait out the heat of the midday sun. I have no head or legs; my body is a ripe carmine, an unsheathed lipstick tunnelling through silken sands. The aureole grains—too light to be called safety-yellow—dribble from my ridges when I emerge. I am so poisonous that to touch me is instant death to any animal. I can shoot venom from bulging sacs under the face I don't have. Imagine that —no face. No eyes, no mouth, no mask to disguise my real emotions. I don't tell lies. I don't tell the truth, either, but the sand covers a multitude of sins.

Despite what you've heard, I cannot shock my

prey using electrical stimuli. That was just a rumour, drummed up by locals. Not everything you see or hear is true. Out here, it may seem possible—even plausible —but let me assure you that I rely solely on the twin powers of poison and venom.

Your approach foments ripples in the ground, grooves on a record cutting too deeply to be heard. Halt, lest you stray too far from hearth and home. A candle often gutters before extinguishing itself; a warning, wick bent sideways like a beckoning finger, before being snuffed out into absence.

Desist.

Do not pour the glass of wine.

Do not invite me to sit down.

Do not beg me, soundlessly, to linger.

Do not glance at the clock.

Do check your phone.

Do reply to your wife's last text.

Do fetch my jacket.

Do stand and usher me out.

You seem assured that these offerings—iron-wrought, clanging praise, and sugar-shy compliments — will be well-met, received with french speckles and wild rosettes and a lolling dip from left to right, but I recognize the tango swoop of slow, meticulous rot, fluffing over one mottled fruit at a time. Braided halters, consisting of words strung up on a single long hair, line your walls, drooping like elderly chins. These harnesses are no more sweet than my venom sacs; they pain the victim just as much. I'm certain you've laid awake wondering how my poison feels. I can tell you it tastes like rusted casket hinges, feels the last shriek of tangled hooves disappearing under sun-washed fur. The green taste of scissors snipping. The sound of cold butter.

Here is the bedroom. Yes. I see that, with the eyes I don't have. I consent, with the mouth I don't have. I smile, with the face I don't have. And you insist on having me, even though I am nothing and mean nobody and afterwards you will be nowhere and will feel no one. A molten candle, moulted down to a stub.

Listen, man-who-wishes-to-be-a-stranger. If I am a Mongolian Death Worm, then you are a descending finger.

PARADISE LOST

He is a cruelly handsome man, with eyes like Brad Pitt and a mouth like a massacre. She is a cruelly beautiful woman, with hair like Sofia Vergara and eyes like late-stage syphilis. I sit across from them in a moderately-priced Italian restaurant and study my laminated menu.

When the waiter arrives, Emelie orders for me. Ken takes longer to decide, as he always does, before inevitably ordering the lasagna. At the beginning of our relationship, I found this rather cute. Lately, it's been irritating me.

Emelie puts her arm around his shoulder as her foot slides up my thigh under the table. "So, darling, how's work?"

"Fine," he says, and I repress the urge to mouth the words along with him. "Same old, same old."

"And you, sweetheart?" Curious grey eyes map out each feather and flake of my face. I wilt under the intensity of her scrutiny. "You've been awfully quiet this last week."

"You have a magical sidekick who is both immensely powerful and stubbornly unhelpful," I say.

She nods. "Trouble with your colleagues again, huh?"

It's not that I don't care about both of them. We've been a throuple for several months now, and I've enjoyed most of it. Perhaps I'm just not cut out for longevity. My eggs sing inside me, seeking new pastures. I want so badly to overturn my nature, to nest with my mates in a more stable environment. I picture the younglings—two or three at most, any more would be difficult to handle—rooting around Ken and Emelie's apartment, skittering across their hardwood floors, bleating for sustenance at the large dining table. It's a nice thought, but the time has come to make a decision. Migration is not always a physical act, after all. "You decide, against all common sense, to fondle any old random magical artefact you come across. This awakens something dreadful which will then hunt you for the remainder of your life, which you will spend fondling yet more magical artefacts." I pause before I add, "You've learned nothing from the experience, and you never will."

She straightens, jabbing an elbow into Ken's side. He blinks. "Wait. Are you unhappy? Because if you are, we can change. The lines of communication are open and ready. Just tell us what you need." He forces a smile, but I can hear nerves twanging underneath. Violin strings, plucked, not bowed.

I shift in my seat. "You've been chosen to participate in a widely-broadcast death game, and so has your love interest, whom you've never spoken to."

"It hasn't been easy for us to decipher your meanings, you know." He's pouting, an expression which looks surprisingly good on his handsome, strong-jawed face. "Like, if all you can talk about lately are YA plot lines then it's not always evident what the subtext—"

"Not that the language barrier is an issue—" Emelie shoots him a look.

"No, of course not," he corrects hastily, and leans back. "I'm not as good with this stuff as Em is. But I'm trying, sweetheart. Doesn't that count for something?"

"Everyone around you has been organized into groups based on one sole personality type, yet you are special and possess attributes from multiple groups."

"Thank you for saying that," she reaches for my claw, stroking tenderly. "We care about you a great deal too."

I sigh. Underneath the table, my dark feathers are moulting onto the floor. "Every adult you know dies or is worse than useless. You, a child, are required to lead an insurgency, rebellion, or revolution, despite being surrounded by military leaders and people with decades of political experience."

"You're breaking up with us?" Ken gapes.

Emelie retracts her hand. They fall silent.

"You've been paired up to work with someone who embodies the opposite character traits. You will fall in love, however implausible this seems." I rise from the table.

They exchange glances. "If that's really how you feel—" His eyes are glistening.

She swallows hard. "We'll miss you. Call us any time. We'd love to stay friends."

I exit the restaurant and watch them through the window for a moment, feeling a deep ache in my chest. The temptation to take it all back is so strong, I almost succumb, but I know I can't give into the weakness. I trace their outline on the window with one wing, but my breath fogs up the glass and they disappear from view. I draw a small heart and leave before the breeze erases the shape.

"You are the chosen one," I whisper into the wind, "and you must save the world."

GRAVITY IN ARMENIA

nce upon a time, in a land only a shadow's width away, three apples fall from the sky and fall upon the ground with soft, plump thuds; one for the writer, one for the storyteller, one for the listener.

The story has always been inside you, nestled amongst hundreds of thousands of tiny tales balled up in your bones, spawning in your blood, clanking through your frontal lobes. The order in which they are picked is entirely random. Chaos, at a narrative level, only exists before the first word is spoken. After that, the story seeds green, sprouts yellow, blooms red. Primary beats are often picked out in polished vertebrae. Characters chitter between frozen teeth, while plots pulse through swollen, dust-dry gums.

The first apple is red; a smooth, glossy scarlet. No pale streaks here—it shines like a drop of carmine blood. The brown stem is an upright, salted forearm, hard to prise from the branch, often requiring bribery and blackmail and broken nails yet prized all the more for the sweated toil and trouble. This branch, contrary to all common sense, grows underground, and ripens only when your back is turned. To catch a red apple is a glorious achievement; to slice one open, hold a knife to your own throat and catch all the lies that seep out. To bear the pain beyond the twisted rings, until nothing but truth sings high and clear, is a journey too difficult for most to bear. Most never even try.

In space, we're pillars of stars, we are beams of light. In space, we expand and contract like lungs made of nothing, like atoms waving to each other from such a great distance that if you were to speak I could not hear you. Yet we are close—so close, in fact, that you could not slide the skin of an atom between us, like greeting one another in the mirror; only a breath of silver to separate us from our other selves. Planet-side, light moves sluggishly, like poured syrup, sticky and sweet on the eyes. Bright on the tongue.

The second apple is a deep sea-green. People plough and die in water worlds; they furrow and live on ice planets, and yet we know nothing of their names, their dynasties, their passions. The ocean is a twisted, untamed leviathan, smooth and colubrine, rapidly swallowing up our hills and glens. A good storyteller handles the green apple with the utmost care, passes the apple from hand to hand and mouth to mouth. The stem of the green apple is a human tongue; the apple survives as long as the stem waggles. When the stem stills, the apple dies, and the story dies with it. Resurrections are rare—not impossible, but rare as true beauty.

On earth, we are temperate objects—tepid under the weight of water, roiling with the colour of memories, the kind of hyacinth that is fathoms deep. On earth, a story never stays still, but naturally moves from a region of high narrative concentration to a region of low narrative concentration. A thrusting stake through the heart of a silent campfire, fizzing and spluttering into life with all the effervescence of a drunken sunrise.

The third apple is bronze—it glows as if lit from inside, as if it was smithed by Hephaestus himself. The black stem is an exact replicate of your own heart, familiarly strange, like meeting a parent's long-lost identical twin. If you press your ear to the chambers you can hear every crack and break ever endured, looping in an endless healing cycle. The third apple is alive. When you hold it in your hand for too long, the amber light consumes you, piece by piece, absorbing your body through the skin until you too are made of apple and you too can see all the patchwork colours of a story, stitched together by burnt-copper thoughts. Here you may also see the outline of yourself, silhouetted in every breath you've yet to take. Only the hardest of hearts can resist falling in love with their shadows all over again.

It was wrong to say that the story is inside you, any more than your sentience is inside you. A necessary deceit. In truth, you are the story, writing each new word with every inhale and exhale. Every cell division is a fresh full stop or a blank space; every newborn blood cell or neural pathway striking a tabbed indent or a paragraph. Every memory a sentence, every moment a page. A library of a lifetime, bound in flesh, and you are the only one who will ever write it, read it, fully appreciate the nuances and the texture and the footnotes of your own existence.

You see, my child, we are all the story within a story, and we must tell of ourselves each and every day. To die a first death is nothing. To die a second death—your name and the effects of your labour fading from the world—is much more permanent.

Isn't that something? Isn't that wild and stormy and beautiful and lonely and far, far too much? To be a person is to be a language few can read, and even less can understand. A language with only one native speaker. Be kind to those who try to form your words, halting over strange trains of consonants, mouthing unusual vowels. They did not grow up knowing you, with intimate access to those dark corners. Those lines that, even now, you are reading between. Do not allow the arrogance of the homelander to fence you off from the larger realm; we have so few ways to connect to each other through space and time, and such a little life as any bright spark can expect before a final flare.

Know. Be known. *Understand.* Make yourself understood. *Love, and permit yourself to be loved.* Tell your stories, and tell them true.

ACKNOWLEDGEMENTS

Firstly, I'd like to thank Nate Ragolia, who fell in love with a caged *Turducken* stuck in a no-fly zone and gave it wings to soar once more. You're my hero, pal.

To my darling fiancée Zebib, who supports me through frequent and ridiculous bouts of workaholism, and who inspires me every day to be a better person—thank you for always being my first reader and my gifted writer-bestie.

To my six incredibly talented and wonderful mentees—Allison, Annie, Anya, Amalie, Kelly, and Laura—thank you for helping me become a better teacher and for trusting me with your work. I'll be buying your books someday, I've no doubt.

To the friends who heard me say "I bet I can put a live chicken inside a live duck inside a live turkey and make you care about it emotionally", and egged me on —pun intended—thank you. To the friends who read multiple stories about this throuple and asked "is it weird if I ship them, though?"—thank you. To the friends who adored the literary pieces in this collection, who used these stories in classes as teaching tools or shared them with friends and community—thank you. I hope to always be worthy of your praise and attention.

Finally, to my fantastic blurbers, Ai Jiang, K.C Mead-Brewer, and Jeffrey Ford—it was an honour and a privilege to have you comment on my work. I am eternally grateful and forever in your debt.

ABOUT THE AUTHOR

Lindz McLeod is a queer, working-class, Scottish writer who dabbles in the surreal. Her short stories have been published by Apex, Catapult, Flash Fiction Online, Pseudopod, and many more. Her longer work includes the novelette LOVE, HAPPINESS, AND ALL THE THINGS YOU MAY NOT BE DESTINED FOR (Assemble Media, 2022), and her debut novel BEAST is forthcoming with Brigids Gate Press in August '23. Lindz writes in English, Scots, and—haltingly—Gaelic. She is a full member of the SFWA, the newly elected Club President of the Edinburgh Writers' Club, and is represented by Laura Zats at Headwater Literary Management. She lives in Edinburgh with her extremely photogenic fiancée and two extremely photogenic cats, Fitzwilliam and Dane. You can follow her on Twitter @lindzmcleod or find out more from her website, www.lindzmcleod.co.uk.

ABOUT THE PUBLISHING TEAM

Nate Ragolia is a lifelong lover of science fiction and its power to imagine worlds more hopeful and inclusive than the real one. His first book, *There You Feel Free*, was published by 1888's Black Hill Press in 2015. Spaceboy Books reissued it in 2021. He's also the author of *The Retroactivist*, published by Spaceboy Books. He founded and edited *BONED*, a literary magazine, has created webcomics, and pets dogs.

Shaunn Grulkowski has been compared to Warren Ellis and Phillip K. Dick and was once described as what a baby conceived by Kurt Vonnegut and Margaret Atwood would turn out to be. He's at least the fifth best Slavic-Latino-American sci-fi writer in the Baltimore metro area. He's the author *Retcontinuum*, and the editor of *A Stalled Ox* and *The Goldfish* for 1888/Black Hill Press.

Printed in Great Britain
by Amazon